How t  Story ɪ nat Doesn't Exist

ENIT'AYANFE AYOSOJUMI AKINSANYA

IFEÁDIGO PUBLISHING COMPANY

Abuja, Nigeria.

2022

1

How to Catch a Story That Doesn't Exist

By Enit'ayanfe Ayosojumi Akinsanya

Layout: IfèAdigo

Contents

Dedication	3
Praises	6
Blurb	11
Disclaimer	12
Now and Forever	13
WhatsApp Voicenotes	31
Bar Boy	49
Half of a Yellow Akamu	78
Tell Mama You Like Boys	100
Hunting for Fireflies: A Grasp at a Fading Sanity	107
Generation to Generation	118
Gilbert	135
The Banishment	146
When We Stop	160
Fate	205
Acknowledgements	224
About the Author	228

DEDICATION

This is for the children called "bruised", who *are* bruised,

whose many stories were never told.

Then for Char Lee Nonso,

who tended this book like a pregnancy.

And for my parents,

Grace and Samuel Akinsanya,

my own stars, my beautiful beginnings, my sustaining middle, my pillars for life—in body and in spirit.

E ò níí s'àsedànù.

In Memoriam

Ananwureyi Joy, "Namie", Queen Ohine.

Perhaps you would have loved to read this.

Rubygold Olamide (or "Scribbled Pen"),

a potent blue memory.

You *loved* my timeline stories. I'm positive you would have loved this, too.

Jude Anuoluwa,

eternal star,

whose stories should have ruled.

And Akachi.

We remember.

"If you ask me for book recommendations and I don't add 'How to Catch a Story that Doesn't Exist' to the list, slap me! Slap me hard!" — *Jax Dey Para*

"[Here is a writer who] deserves awards. I admire the way he writes, and his boldness. I love this." — *Desmond (Ben) Chidera Udeh,* author of the classic novel, *"People for Rent"*

"Enit'ayanfe Ayosojumi is not just talented; he is also skilled. Reading this gave me the atmosphere of reading Adichie's and Achebe's works. And when can we please talk about his fearless "in their face" chronicling of taboo experiences? Fierce." — *Chidi Ebirim*

"Rich in domesticated proverbs, a reminiscence of Chinua Achebe's literary works. A most courageous revelation of the most dreaded perspectives of the African society." — *Olusegun Moses Alli*

"[These stories are] filled with an applaudable courage. The most exciting thing is the descriptive power. [Ayosojumi] writes so well, in fact sometimes like Alan Hollinghurst. Well done." — *Ebelenna Tobenna Esomnofu,* author of the award-winning book, *"Madness"*

"Enit'ayanfe's talent is amazing. [This book] gave everything it was supposed to give. I'm still in awe!" — *Tlhompho Kgatla*

"I could not keep calm. I was barely ten pages in and yet I already couldn't keep calm. Enit'ayanfe's tropes in these stories are so real, so relatable, and so original. This is the most positively manipulative and intriguing book I've read in a while. The world has been blessed with a powerful writer and it's Ayosojumi." — *Simply Preye*

"This is too good." — *Ugochukwu Anadi*

"I recommended this to my friends here in Kenya! Such sweetness." — *Njoki Maina*

"I've not before read something as deep and as detailed as 'How to Catch a Story that Doesn't Exist'. It gives life and voice to realities silent but present in our society. A very beautiful, very brave collection." — *Templeton Ugochukwu Peetarh*

"I found some of the stories very poetic, a striking resemblance to Ben Okri's work. Thank you [Enit'ayanfe] for writing this wonderful book. If I could go back in time to change one thing, it would be to gift my teenage self this book." — *Chibuike Agbo Kingsley*

"Ayosojumi knows how to capture and propel you into a story. He is a born writer." — *Deemusah*

"I am not surprised. Every time [Ayosojumi] holds the pen, it bleeds with love, passion and a fierce, fearless reality." — *Martins Anumene*

"A page-turner. A must read. [Ayosojumi] did a wonderful job." — *Titi Tst Bauer*

"A surreal accomplishment that froze me from read to read. It didn't help that I related to most of the stories with a hard-hitting precision." — *Yusuf J Nasadau Galadima*

"Enit'ayanfe Ayosojumi has a way of capturing hearts when he puts these stories out there. He is a wonder." — *Osas Angela Egharevba*

"The synergy among the characters is intense!" — *Kenneth Amobi*

"This book is nothing short of a rollercoaster. By turns happy and critical and agonizing. It took me through different worlds. […] I went through the darkest tunnel and found light at the end of it. I finally felt like a hero. I can't wait for more titles from Ayosojumi!" — *Hrh Temitope-Oluwa Gabriels*

"What joy." — *Meziem Janet*

"Enit'ayanfe is a god!" — *Faithfulness David*

"After so long, I finally read this. Every story was like a delicious meal. It bit subtly into my soul. I could taste every emotion. And then the unexpected abundance of hope and laughter! Enit'ayanfe Ayosojumi Akinsanya is a significant storyteller, a great raconteur. Can't wait for him to be recognized in Africa—in fact, the whole world!" — *Ement Amaku*

"I don't repeat books but I am going to repeat this." — *Daerego Ekine*

"What a timely appearance in our literary world! [Enit'ayanfe] meticulously penned down the truth we are afraid to speak. This is an indispensable guide to discovering us, a pinch bringing us (back) to reality. Thank [you] Ayo." — *Peter Anikpe*

"This was almost perfect!" — *Kingsley Sunshine*

"Ayosojumi wrote about the life I want and the life I do not want. I got mixed feelings; I was sad and nervous and hopeful. This is value itself. This book is real life." — *Femi Uzor*

"Intriguing. Educating. Everyone should read this." — *Ayodele Abegunde*

"A rattling read. Through a powerful imagery and an undeniable witchery of words, [this] shines! From the very first story, the characters came alive before me! How does [Ayosojumi] do this?" — *Kingsley Alfred*

"Vivid. Breath-taking. It's my first book of such content. I hope it won't be the last." — *Crystal Adeniji*

"With this, Ayosojumi came already refined." — *Felix Godwin*

"[Stories] of love, despise, ruin, beauty and inseparability, suffused with all the innocence and originality in the world. Amazing." — *Egboka Victory*

"One of the best I've come across." — *Kenny Bell*

"A monumental, very bold work. The language is so unapologetically clear I watched it unravel." — *Zealy Owen*

"This genius of a literary work is an almost unbearable reminder of our deepest taboo human struggles—and few human triumphs." — *Minato Osem*

"The latter [part] had me flying through sentences, running through words to find out what happened. The writer's descriptive power is poignant and razor-sharp. A beautiful diction, too. More of this, please." — *Umeh Chisom*

"This is refreshing." — *John Agu*

"[Enit'ayanfe] created the exact picture!" — *Okorie Onyekachi Paul*

"So beautiful. I wanted the stories to have sequels." — *Ogbonna Uchenna*

"[Enit'ayanfe] took me from the present world and led me to the gritty one he wrote about. I was like a spectator and everything was happening around me. Only few writers can do that to me. Thank you!" — *Martins Dale Ogbe*

"The writing style easily made a connection between the reader and the writer. I feel so blessed looking into Ayosojumi's soul." — *Elkanah*

"Many emotions rushed through me all at once!" — *Moses J. Karima*

"Enit'ayanfe's imagery paints a very hypnotic capture for readers' attention till the last word. This is full mastery on display and I hope he doesn't spare us in the future. These stories are goosebumps-inducing!" — *Benyin Ogar*

"This is just too good. I love what I read." — *Ogiis Emmanuel*

"Great writing!" — *Giftluv Rhianna*

"Ayosojumi says things we only wish we could express. A staggeringly daring feat, especially considering the country he comes and writes from." — *Steve Crane*

"Enit'ayanfe Ayosojumi really has a way with words. I smelt and felt creativity all around. Each storyline itself was a hook; it struck me. Enit'ayanfe is a strong voice for us all." — *Japhet Ozii*

"There's something a good work of art does to you. It envelops you, consumes you whole and never leaves you until you're done appeasing it in the way it wants to be appeased. My eyes didn't blink for a second; they were glued to the world [Enit'ayanfe] created to the last word. It's beautiful, so beautiful. The diction is simple, original, deep. We are grateful for this book." — *Sochukwuma Ijem*

BLURB

How to Catch a Story That Doesn't Exist is a collection of eleven stories that depict what time, tradition and decision can do to the relationships that are most elemental to us, in a world that constantly works to tear us into shreds.

In "WhatsApp Voicenotes", an extremely paranoid university student suffering from an unnamed acute illness weaves a tapestry of suicidal fantasies that lead him to a truth he is not prepared to look at.

Two girls grow into womanhood in "Generation to Generation", split by the mishaps of their childhood. Decades later, their children are to meet a similar fate, under permanently sealed, delicate conditions.

A family travels down from different parts of the world in "When We Stop" and meets at their old aunt's house to celebrate their parents' wedding anniversary. Are they ready to look beyond the hurts and failures of their past and the unallayed fears of the present, and forge forward as the family they are?

And in the story from which the title of the collection is drawn, "Half of a Yellow Akamu", a boy fantasizes about his much older crush, who ignores him. Things get messy when his cousin discovers his secret desire and torments him with it, even as the harsh realities of the aftermath of the 1967-1970 Nigeria-Biafra war seek to suck them in.

These stories, riddled with intrigue, suspense, danger and poignancy, with its unforgettable characters, will remain with you long after you've read the last page.

DISCLAIMER

One of the stories, "The Banishment", was first published under the same title in The Shallow Tales Review Magazine, 34th Edition [July, 2021].

NOW AND FOREVER

The fight was fucking intense. At first, no blows were thrown, no punches delivered, no weaponizing. Just both of them tackling each other. Grabbing. Scratching. Each bent on overthrowing the other, like opponents at an *ijakadi* bout. They were on the bedroom balcony, spacious enough for an arena, bright with the glare from the afternoon sun. At their feet, Lekki Phase One slept, wrapped in silence, all souls enclosed in a cavalcade of high walls and impersonal mansions, their roofs blazing. The fighters lived alone in their duplex. Just Tunmise, really, because Dare only stayed in during strikes and holidays. And although Tunmise's father owned many oil wells on The Mainland and much landed property on The Island, the man hardly stayed in Lagos. He was always flying to Port Harcourt or Indonesia or wherever else for business deal closures. That was his style, even before his wife died of diabetes. The woman made him vow, in her last hours, that he was going to be there for their children, no matter how busy he got. It wasn't a difficult thing at all then, to give out one of his Lagos properties to Tunmise on Tunmise's insistence to live alone after his NYSC programme. There was ceaseless Wi-Fi supply, there were well-stocked liquor chests; there were all the things that made a house feel like a deluxe hotel. This meant that Tunmise was free to engage his "clients", bill them with overused "formats" to add figures he didn't really need to his pocket money (an endless ritual from his father, as "lastborn indulgences") and bring as many men home as he liked. Dare was not one of those men. Dare was different. It was the appearance of Dare in his life that barricaded the entrance to the other men—and the women, too. Dare was the only one Tunmise had ever slid into without a condom, the only one who had beaten him at FIFA 21 repeatedly on PS5, the only one who did not walk around Tunmise on tiptoe nor whisper over Tunmise's wealth. Dare behaved like a wild cat, enough wildcatness to transform Tunmise, an intrinsically gentle man, into another serious wildcat. Tunmise sometimes regretted loving it that way.

Like he did this particular day. Had his brothers been in Nigeria with him, and not stuck like teeth in London with his old aunt, one of them would be with him in the house, or at least be present on the day of the fight, and so would have controlled things. And perhaps, just perhaps, Dare wouldn't have found what he found in his drawer.

"Let me go to that drawer," Dare said now. He puffed and strained like an adder, his eyes wild with promised consequences.

"I *no fit*. See, I don't want you to get hurt again." Tunmise held him fast to his chest, a lifeline that, if let go, spelled doom. He would rather jump through the teeth of a shark than let Dare get to that drawer. "So I won't. I'm protecting you." He should have locked the damn thing. Or better still, destroyed the—

"What's your business with that? Have I ever asked for your protection? Free me! *Hmm*. Tunmise, you know me. You know me *o*! Free me *jeje* now and let me get to that drawer before I dance with my grandfather's masquerade."

"Haa, don't dance with your grandfather's masquerade." Tunmise tried to heave him off his feet and carry him downstairs. It surprised him, how a body that had

14

been squishily amenable against him the previous night had now easily transformed into a solid unyielding mass.

"*Fi mi si'le!*" Dare wailed. "Let me go!"

"No!"

Dare slammed a hand across his own brow and let out a groan. "Oluwatunmise! You know the things that get me mad! Okay, wait, *wait*. What are you hiding in that drawer? What are you hiding there?"

"Nothing. It doesn't even matter. I mean—"

"It doesn't matter! Yet, you are gripping me *ni papamora* as if we're doing standing doggy!"

"Ha! Standing doggy *bawo?*"

"Oluwatunmise Olamiposi, son of Engineer Olagbaju Olanbiwonninu Odufeso."

"Sir!"

"You started when I dropped my face cream on that drawer this morning. Why? Why did you look worried? What are you hiding?"

"Something I should have removed."

Dare went stiff in his arms, that lull just before the eruption of lava from a fissured volcano. An airplane droned past and they glanced toward the lofty roof.

"Jesus Christ. What's that? What's the thing you should have done? You said no more secrets. What did you keep away from me?"

Tunmise's lips were a flat resolve.

Dare's eyebrows, overly shaped, went up. "Is it the G-string of one of your useless Bottoms?"

Tunmise gasped. "Is that how low you think of me?"

"No. But you leave me with so many questions."

"Your questions should have a range." Tunmise's eyes became cloudy. Blood thrummed through his head, but he managed to hold on to his patience. "You know I would never act like that towards you."

Dare relaxed against the wall of flesh behind him, with a sigh. "I know you'd never act like that towards me."

"So cut me some slack. Don't irritate me with your questions."

Dare rolled his eyes. "Daddy *wa*. I will irritate you with questions. I will! What are you hiding? My mouth is tired of asking that question."

"N-nothing."

"My God! Nothing?" Dare's eyes were dilated; he looked ready to shriek the whole estate awake.

"Nothing deliberate this time, I swear. I really didn't mean to, er—shit! I swear on my mother's grave!"

"Don't swear o. Leave the woman to rest *abeg*. Keeper of secrets!"

Tunmise blinked twice. "What?"

"Let me go to that drawer!"

Tunmise tightened his hold. "I won't."

The furious fumbling resumed, drifted from the balcony back into the bedroom, the same bedroom that had absorbed their cries of ecstasy the night before. They struggled past the curtains. Dare lunged a back kick into Tunmise's shin. He chuckled when Tunmise's hands

16

slackened around his torso. Dare was the fitter one. He had a gym card that he used regularly. He had also participated in a series of prayer walks on the Babcock University campus, where he was in his final year, reading Business Management. But prayer walks were not enough, had never been enough, for a Nigerian like him. So he had joined a secret off-campus judo class to be—in his words—"more practical and more intentional about my protection in a country like this". Now, he was lithe, abundantly agile and nimble. And could kick some ass. Even if it was going to be his boyfriend's.

Tunmise howled, limped loose and melted to the floor. He watched Dare race for the chest of drawers next to the massive bed, a sturdy mahogany affair that had—to their shock—actually creaked under their simulations and ejaculations the previous night. "No!" he screamed like an actor, spread helplessly on his knees as though sucked to the cold tiled floor.

But Dare had already yanked the top drawer open, his eyes snapping with suspense. To his deflation, he found *Genevieve* and *City People* magazines lying open over each other. The polished, sculpted faces of the Kardashians beamed up at him. In one corner, Beyoncé's hair flew, haloing the microphone she held. He shrugged the disappointment off. There *was* something else. His fingers worked swiftly—nothing, nothing but the little dust on the gloss. Tunmise made a small movement. Dare glanced at him. On the bed was Tunmise's Apple MacBook, white, light, fragile, open, still blinking on his Cash App page. Dare raised a finger to warn him. He wouldn't smash his laptop, of course, that would be a little extra, but he raised the finger still. Then he reached for the middle drawer and dragged it out. It was full of condom packs and lube packets. He rummaged through the jumble, paused, looked up and pulled out a piece of paper. A deadly missive from the touch of it, carefully folded in quarters. Only Tunmise could have folded it that neatly. He did things with a graceful calibration; when his head was between Dare's thighs, he sucked with that same carefulness.

Dare sat on the bed, opened the paper and read it. He was a little surprised that Tunmise was still crouched on the floor, not making any more desperate moves, not trying to wrest the paper from his hands, just panting and panting, like a dog that played too much. Another sharp glance at Tunmise's face midway into the letter explained everything: the Rubicon had been crossed; there was no use trying to stop Dare now; the letter was already in his hands, the content deepening into the cotton of his mind.

Silence tiptoed around the commodious room, for a lifetime. Only the A/C hummed. Tunmise stood slowly.

Dare finished reading the letter and mechanically folded it back, as it had been. His fingers twitched. They had twitched like that in secondary school when he glimpsed his ex-boyfriend, a student from the senior class, kissing the Head Girl in front of the dormitory's bathroom, weeks away from their Valedictory Service. He couldn't copy his notes down properly in WASSCE lesson class. He was not sure what had struck him more: that his boyfriend was kissing a girl, or that the kissing had happened on the forbidden premises of the male hostel's bathroom. His hands had twitched for days.

"I can explain," Tunmise intoned, stepping close and drawing back sharply when Dare raised a warning hand, again. Don't come near me, the hand said. Don't.

"Baby, please, I can explain. At least hear me out first." Tunmise was practically wringing his hands.

Dare nodded slightly to show that he was not holding his tongue; he should get on with it.

"I am no longer seeing her. I swear. I am no—"

"You told me you blacklisted her number and blocked her on all social media handles."

"Yes, I did."

"But now, here is a letter…" Dare raised the damning sheet "…a very new letter…to her."

"Just listen to me. She called me again, using somebody's line, and said she was sorry for what she did. I got a little annoyed with her; no, not because she called me again after telling her off the last time, but because she thought I was still mad at her. Of course, I am not mad at her. I can't be. I never loved her anyway. I just thought I did. She was not Anita; she couldn't be." He patted his own cheeks and sighed. "Since Anita died in that blasted Dana crash, I hadn't felt the same. I thought I would never be alive again. Then we met inside that Shoprite and I spilled my cappuccino on your shirt and you almost screamed my head off and, even as I apologized, I knew, I just knew I was going to be spilling more stuff on you."

"Oh shut up." Dare nudged the flirting away. But a smile desperately tugged at his lips.

Tunmise gazed down at the floor for a while. He was silent for so long that Dare guiltily thought that he was crying. He could. He was an *Ajebutter* after all. Those bourgeois luxury-laden Lagos kids always turned things into drama, and then recoiled in wide-eyed shock when they saw real drama coming for their heads.

Tunmise spoke. "You are the closest thing to Anita, and yet there is this difference to you, like a bonus." He raised his eyes; there were no tears in them; rather, they gleamed with something more emotional than tears. "Why are you doing this to me, D.? I would never play you like a ball. Yes, I like girls, too, and I will still like girls and will always like girls. But being with you gives me something I can't explain. I've begun to wonder why I'm so focused on you. I'm supposed to be bisexual. *I'm* bisexual."

Dare's eyebrows met firmly. "Why are you astonished at yourself? Bisexuality is not when you are dating both cis genders at the same time, Tunmise. *That*'s bigamy. Muhammad doesn't cheat on his girlfriend, does he? I know people don't exactly stamp it on their foreheads, but I have eyes for such a thing. You remember how all those sexy naked Tops were lining up to feel him up when he was twerking to 'Anaconda' at that Christmas party we threw at Elegushi Beach. You and I know where he drew the line. And I know many more monogamous bisexuals, so don't even start. And could you please for God's sake stop comparing me with Anita?"

"*Hmm*," Tunmise hummed, fighting the urge to flinch. Dare had been just as forceful at a social club when a newly introduced friend said, smiling, "Your Boo has told us a lot about you, Dare. I'm straight, but I can still move with sensible and good-looking gays like you." "Boy, please. You must think of that as a compliment, huh? But I'm here to break the news to you that it's in fact not. I'm not a showglass product, if that's what you think. And it's rich of you to assume I want to move with folks like *you*," Dare had fired back and Tunmise's friend had held his tongue throughout the hangout.

"Have you been listening to that nonsense boy on Facebook?" Tunmise asked now.

"Which nonsense boy on Facebook?"

"You know who." He tapped Dare on the nose, quickly, feinting, before Dare could slap his hand away.

"I don't know who." Dare shrugged. "I don't need to listen to any nonsense boy on Facebook before I know what nonsense is. Imagine me sleeping with someone else now and saying it is because I'm attracted to men. *Haba.* People are people and, in a relationship, you cannot blame whatever wrong they do on sexual orientation. You blame it on personal traits. Which means y'all have to stop saying stuff like, well, that you only seem selfish because you swing both ways, because that's not why. And it actually gives you bad rep." He stared into Tunmise's eyes. "Haven't I told you I would like to kiss your cousin, the hot one who recently flew in from London, whose skiing pictures you once posted on IG? You also know about how he propositioned me after I went to his PM and said 'Hi, just want to say you look real cute. I'm your cousin's boyfriend.' He must have thought I was flirting, when I was only complimenting him. I told you, didn't I? I didn't go behind your back. It's because it's something I will never do. It was a simple courtesy." He gently poked Tunmise's chest. "Now, *that* was transparency. Transparency is really important, Mr. Man; don't go sneaking around."

Tunmise rocked on his feet, his shoulders jerking, his head thrown back. "D.! D.!"

"What?"

"I hear you, sir."

"Better."

Tunmise shook his head, an indulgent smile holding his lips open. "Do you know my guys call me 'brave'? When you're away in school and we're all hanging out with their girls and they ask after you, they say, 'T-Fundz, how's your Wild Cat?' I often forget that you are indeed *wahala*. It must be *jaz*. You used your people's jaz on me, Ogun boy."

Dare flung a palm. "Please, don't be ridiculous. Like Ogun state is the only place known for juju. What about you Lagosians that are always going naked or wearing white and washing nonsense into the lagoon? *Biko* tell your *amebo* friends to mind their business. They are not my boyfriend o."

But that hint of a smile taunted his lips still. He held the paper like a shield, got up and walked down outside to the porch, down to the hibiscus block in the middle of the sprawling compound, close to where he parked his Lexus. He yearned to grasp something solid.

Tunmise followed him and sat on the block's edge. The block burned his buttocks. He winced. "Bring it, let me tear it."

Dare's fingers fastened ferociously around the letter. "*Why* are you keeping it? You said she called you with a line; why didn't you just text it to her straight? This is 2020. Who the fuck writes letters these days?"

"Oluwadamilare. When you're here and we quarrel and go for days without speaking to each other, what do I do?"

Dare rolled his eyes. "You write."

"And?"

22

"Then you convert your writings to texts and send them to me."

"Good. Because I find it easier to write. When I try to speak or type, I leave out too many things. I only remember more long after I've spoken or typed. Writing is my best mode of communication, honestly."

"Well, I've always thought it was romantic anyway, you taking paper and writing so seriously, things you should have just said, and me watching you and you pretending to not know that I'm watching you." He pursed his lips and shook his head. "Don't smile, young man. It's a silly kind of romance, very silly."

"It's romance, still." Tunmise laughed, and it looked as though the flowers became brighter. He rubbed his leg. "Babe, you hit me hard upstairs. *Omo!*"

"I would be damned if I said sorry." Dare looked away.

Tunmise pulled at his arm joshingly. "Why are you like this? That's how you punched Obong in the mouth that night at the club when he said he was going to smash a bottle on my head. You didn't even fear his big muscles! I should find that your judo trainer and lock him up."

Another eye-roll. "You knew I wouldn't let him do that to you. Break a bottle on your head? On top of gini? Was he mad? You didn't seem keen on stopping him, so I did what I had to do. What's there? The fool was hopelessly drunk. Besides, his muscles are useless. I am not one of the people he can beat up. Strategy is also a strength. When I beat people up and make them see me differently, I use strategy. That's what I did with Obong."

"*Na wa!*"

"I wonder how Daniel still manages to be with him *sha*. I'm sure it's because of his yahoo money."

"Omo! Was that why you hit me, too, without mercy eh, your own boyfriend, *olowo ori e*?"

"I am the only one on God's earth allowed to get rough with you. Serves you right! By the way," he bit his lower lip gently and moaned, "you hit me hard last night, too."

"*Chai*. But you didn't complain *nah*. Eh? Instead, you held my waist more tightly and pulled me deeper into you."

Dare held his esophagus and stuck out his tongue. "*Abeg, abeg!* See, I don't want to sound churchy, love, but you're going to hell for saying that."

"I don't mind any hell o, as long as I've at least had the chance to live and be with you." He reached for Dare's nose again and pulled at it. "Being with you is like heaven."

"*Mo fo o.*" Dare laughed. "You have started. Men and their sweet mouths."

"It's your self-drag for me. Aren't you one, too? Do you even recall all the things you say when your eyes are shut and I'm moving? You once said you were going to buy me a plot of land on Banana Island. Where is it?"

"*Oniro!* Liar! I made no such promises. I don't care what the height of orgasm may be *o*; I can never open my mouth and say rubbish like that. You rate yourself too highly!"

"Ha! Really!"

"Yes, darling!"

"You'll come back."

"*For where?* Look at you. I'm carrying my bag tomorrow and going back. You didn't hear? The second lockdown has been relaxed."

"Chai." It dawned on him like the setting of the sun on an empty village. He felt his chest crumple with loss. Each time he insisted on dropping Dare off at school and knowing where Dare was and what Dare was doing, it was because his heart jumped. His heart jumped because Dare was a smart, fine boy who spoke his mind, and Dare's expressiveness could be misinterpreted by the campus men as "open for freaky shit". "Who will now cook for me?" he said, making a poor-cat face.

Dare giggled. "Eat out. Or find an idle bitch in the estate."

"I knew you'd say nonsense." Tunmise shrugged. "Anyway, I'll cook for myself."

"Who? You?"

"Yes nah. I'll cook for my belly."

"You can't cook to save your life, Tunmise."

"Stay there o. Is it not to read cookbooks? Once I'm hungry enough, inspiration go come. We *meeuve.*"

Dare laughed. "Wahala be like Inspiration FM. Anyway, I'll make *efo riro* with fresh fish and stock your fridge before I leave."

Tunmise yodeled. "That's my baby. I knew you wouldn't want me starving." He made as if to kiss him.

"Go *jo.* See the way you're touching me anyhow. No social distancing, no sanitizing. Neither of us is even wearing a mask. You want to catch Coro?"

25

"Wetin be Coro?"

"Ahn ahn. Covid-19 nah."

"I know. I'm just asking what it is. You dey believe these people? You don't see them in their white agbadas throwing parties? You think say e dey true-true? Even if it's real, it can't catch people like us. Not after everything we did last night."

"Ah! It is real o, Boo. I don't want to catch Covid-19 *abeg*."

"*Pele o*. How about Covid-96? Come and collect that one." Then he started pecking him on the neck, jaw, shoulders, ducking from each weak slap, then stopping. "I can't wait for you to sign out of that school."

"So that what?" Dare zipped his fingers behind Tunmise's neck; their eyes melded. "Actually, let me admit, I love riding you."

Tunmise gasped. "Damn, Babe. Now who's going to hell!" He mumbled some sweet nothings, tickling Dare, Dare wriggling and hollering. They fumbled around for some time. Then they stopped, wheezing. He took Dare in his arms. "Come here; your fake tattoos are fading. Let me draw new ones. Those pastors in your school *sef*, how did you manage to hide it from them, you rebel?"

"What did you leave out in the letter?"

"Baby?"

Dare was still, too still. "This letter, is there anything else I should know?"

Tunmise stared at him, a half-wounded, half-musing stare. The revving of a car broke the air. Somebody's gates squealed open and the voice of a man said, "Welcome,

26

madam." A dog woofed, rattling its cage. Finally, Tunmise sighed. "There is nothing else you ought to know. But I think I went too far by adding 'two-faced bitch' in the actual text."

The laughter jerked out of Dare in rich spurts. He couldn't hold it in this time, the way it soared gleefully, wickedly, from inside his chest, and merged with Tunmise's, a harmonious blending.

"Sounds like what I say to my *magas* who get another 'African wife' while still with me," Tunmise barked.

Dare clapped. "Mr. Tunmise, T-Fundz Africa, *e* bad *gan*!"

Tunmise hummed.

"Are we going to have to deal with more 'two-faced bitches' or any kind of bitches at all in the future—like, am I just another maga?" Dare asked, half-teasing.

Tunmise's eyes narrowed. "I may be unserious about many things in my life, and I know you scold me daily for whiling away precious time by squeezing money I don't really need from online strangers who swallow my format, at my age. But if there is one thing that takes my entire mind, it is the thought of you. I said you have used jaz on me. I want to marry you. I want to be seeing you every fucking day. You're the love of my life and there's no 'for now' in it."

"Wow." Dare's mouth was an O. "You've never spoken that forcefully about us before."

Tunmise smiled. "I love the way you said 'are we going to have to deal with more two-faced bitches'. It made me feel exactly the way I felt just now when you said 'forcefully

27

about us'." He reached out and held Dare's hand. "I'm no longer a kid, Lare. I know what I want. I mean every word. Look at the letter again, did you get any nuance that I still want to kid around?"

Dare looked at him, at how steady his eyes were, eyes unafraid to say the truth. He sighed, suddenly wishing he had not kicked him. "No," he finally said, "there is none. It was even colder than I expected. I was disappointed when I read it. I'm sorry."

"I must have overreacted then. I shouldn't have tried to block you from getting to the drawer. I just didn't want something so small to ruin this big thing we already have. This is our third year together, *sebi*?"

"Yeah. We need more faith. Fear is bad."

"Come, *wa*," Tunmise said, pulling him close until Dare landed, softly, between his thighs. He pressed his lips against his neck, whispering mumbo-jumbo against it. A million needles shot across Dare's tense nerves and left them tingling with a different rhythm. "*Ma fo*. Let's see what new patterns we can draw on this lovely seamless skin of yours before you go back to that your religious school."

As he nibbled Dare's ear, Dare thought of how Tunmise's eyes had not wavered while he was saying, "You are the love of my life and there's no 'for now' in it." His breathing hastened; his nipples hardened. He tipped his head sideways to escape the befuddling ravaging of those red-hot lips burning holes down his throat, and asked, "What you said on the phone last week, that you wanted to know what I will do after I finish from school, did you mean 'now', like what I would do about my pastor parents and my life, or did you mean you want to see what I would do thereafter, about settling down and pursuing my career?"

Tunmise turned him around, cradled the back of Dare's head on his shoulder and wrapped his arms around him. "When that bridge comes, we'll cross it. Together. For now, let's just breathe. Life is beautiful, and I don't want to ever leave your side." He tightened his embrace, gently. "Damilare, I know you have fears because of your family and what I am and what you have experienced in the past. But, by now, I think you should know how ruthlessly blunt I can be. I am in my late thirties; I know what I want. You have to trust me if we gotta make this thing work. You have to let go of that chain from your past." He closed his lips around Dare's earlobe and breathed gently. Dare moaned and relaxed against him. "If I want to be with a woman in this life, I can and I would. I've been with women, great, sexy, well-mannered, beautiful women who don't give me wahala like you do. But… I don't know. I feel with you this undying vibe I cannot name. It's like I'm eternally curious about you, wondering what next you will do, what next you will be with me. It's like I can always push down obstacles, face anything, just because you are there on the other side. I know I'm not really saying everything, and I'm not even sure I'm making sense here, I wish I could just write and text you this, but I think you know I cannot—"

He stopped. Dare had placed a finger across his lips. Their eyes met in a dizzying bond, and he longed to kiss him.

"Shh, you're rambling, Tunmise. Just say, 'now and forever'."

Tunmise grinned against the finger, an expansive childlike grin that made his pink lower lip appear pinker. "Now and forever, Oluwadamilare." Then he threw his head back and roared. "I would have bitten that finger, you know, gently, like I did last night."

Dare chortled. "You are impossibly naughty! God! Biko, take." He pushed the letter into Tunmise's hand to do with it as he liked.

"Tell me you don't like it!" Tunmise said, and rent the sheet into pieces, pieces so tiny they appeared to Dare like confetti, like they would rise on the wind and float. They did.

"That's that," Tunmise said, gazing into his eyes. He jerked him back though his lap and fastened his lips again on his throat. "Now, boy-o, where were we?"

WHATSAPP VOICENOTES

1.

hi. you will listen to this very calmly; my mind turns upon itself and runs away from me too fast, and I can barely catch it. but if you stay with me, you might get where I am going.and I hope you never get to listen to these anyway.

[a shattering sneeze]

blood? ahh yeah. it's blood quite all right. there're feathers, too.

[another sneeze]

more blood. good.

the hell are these visions—and why have they followed me, from moments I can only describe as "torrid"?

a dangling noose. an old pashmina. a big shiny knife. and a strange bottle with your head on its label.

those are the things I see each time I'm in the lab, when other people are seeing normal things.

I'm sorry pe my voice is shaking. is it weird that I really do not want you to listen to these? you asked me pe ki n tell you why I've not been replying to your chats, and why I avoid your house when I come to Sagamu. I swear it's not because you slept with your neighbor. I knew you would—I had always known pe you would, from the very first day he came and knocked on the door while I was visiting, and you asked him to enter, even though you and I were sitting together and talking.

I've been leaving your chats on read for a different reason.

I can't type. and I don't want my voice to betray me if I call.

funny then pe I'm here speaking into a phone.

[shaky laughter]

I slept naked last night. not pe I want to corrupt your imagination (there is nothing to corrupt anyway; you know the contours of my body), sugbon I slept as I was born last night, in the skin God wrapped around these scatterings that are inside me.

idi? no. not the heat. I wasn't even alone in the room. I just wanted to sleep naked. I had never slept naked. people talk about it, in hungry tones, bi eni pe they're talking about one of the things you must do before you die.

other people want to be cremated and, like poems, be kept in a Grecian urn, or like a desert pilgrim's banjo music, be strewn in the wind.

I would like to be buried naked.

this morning, I went to the bathroom. I couldn't go to any lectures. I peed and it was bright yellow. my roommate said pe it is iba. I have it in my body.

it is six days until Valentine's, and I have iba in my body.

does iba bring crimson mucus from the nose? when we catch malaria fever and sneeze, is it blood that comes out?

[giggles, a severed string of high sounds]

roomie is talking rubbish and he does not know. he says pe the sanest thing to do is to go to the school clinic. I have completed my registration and I have my ID card, don't I? he is wondering why I am just sneezing and looking at the blood. he asked me pe was it money issues; I said, no, it is not money. iba stays for, at most, two weeks in my body; it will leave. he is scared—he's in Pharmacy, wants to sneak sample drugs home to me. sugbon that is not my concern.

my concern ni you, death.

don't be surprised pe I called you death. you *are* my death—my end, my new beginning. I blame you. I blame you for losing me. I blame you for loving a virus like me. nigbati I'm in Sagamu with you and I walk down the long, winding, dusty roads of Kara, alone, where the Hausa butchers and fruit-sellers walk barefoot, their jalamias blowing around their wiry frames, the sun slanting dust motes like awkward halos around their heads, and they call me "yan daudu", and they point at my long hair and dainty walk, and they spit and flash their knives or try to run me over with their wheelbarrows, I blame you for rubbing my back nigbati I return home to you, shaking. I blame you for leaning on clichés, for saying pe everything would be all right.

do you know pe they also call me "nyamiri"? I wonder how they know. was it you who told them? sorry, couldn't be you. is it my hair, my face? is my ethnicity stamped on my body? sugbon I am detribalized. I have always been. I hardly even know the way back home anymore. my best friend in secondary school is Hausa. Garba. he and I used to pick the same table during Biology practical. we swapped lab coats. we lapped each other on the bus ride home. we were equal human beings. so why must somebody insult me for being Igbo? am I supposed to say "I'm sorry I'm Igbo"? my people are not known for that.

I called my aunt and told her about it. she said pe it was normal; was I not supposed to be used to it? she sounded irritated, as though she were busy and I was bothering her with small talk. I told her pe it must be the legacy of a war-torn country. Biafra had happened; therefore I am a rebel by birth. do you know they still blame us for Biafra? she laughed ka-ka-ka-ka on the phone as if I had gone crazy. she said, "when you come visiting, don't they call you 'omeka nwanyi' here, too? why don't you mention Biafra when they do that?" I said that was different. she said why did I think pe that was different? I couldn't say anything. I could have pointed out to her pe 'omeka nwanyi' and 'nyamiri' are not the same thing and so cannot have the same undertone. in the slur hurled at me by the Hausa men over my looks and gestures is the darkness of tribalism. but I was tongue-tied; I let her carry on with her argument. she said pe it is 2020 and no Hausa man would try to run a lone Igbo boy over or stab him, unprovoked, just nitori Biafra. pe it was about my looks and not my history.

I dropped the call.

I have heard the old men and women in my family talk about how the Igbo starved and slept with one eye open and were buried in shallow graves, hastily dug since the bomber planes could appear any moment, an air raid that said, "dammit, you Igbos shouldn't exist!"

Ocho-Okwu from my mother's clan—as old as he is— is still weeping over his sister. she disappeared during the war, days before his kinsmen waved surprisingly green branches for the war ending. he does not know whether she's dead, so that he could finally seal off his grief, or

34

whether she's alive somewhere, grown-up, married and looking for him, too, and so he could keep hoping.

I know the darker nuances of my identity. sugbon I am not even Biafran. I was born years after the war. so how? I was born into Nigeria. maybe that's the only way it became my history.

for us in this generation, could history be things we have personally experienced and still experience, or could history be things we are taught at home and in school by our elders?

away from that—nigbati we make excuses for, or look away from, attack on our difference—any type of difference—are we saying "forget it; it doesn't matter?"

were you, somehow, by rubbing my back and saying mollifying things, agreeing with those who attacked me that I shouldn't exist?

I blame you nigbati they gather against me. I blame you nigbati I walk through streets or go to classes with people's eyes always stuck on my back, my front, every part of me. I blame you for always saying it was okay, for always being so optimistic, for always laughing and spreading light bi eni pe you were a lamp.

2.

you often held my hand on busy roads, especially at Awolowo Market and Sabo and Oja-Oba, with all those tiny okada sluicing past Dangote trucks that in turn lumbered noisily past impatient cars, and—just as we were about crossing—you would say, with a lazy grin, "let's commit suicide." nigbati I cried in the shadow of our intimacy and you held me and laid my head on your chest and rubbed my cheek, you often waited for a moment between my sobs to say, "let's commit suicide", coz you knew pe it would make me laugh out loud. and Friday evening yen nigbati you hugged me real close and said we should kuku meet very early the next morning outside campus and take a bus to the Lagos-Benin expressway, where we would run into a speeding car and end it all, I was laughing inside nitori I knew you were dry-joking as usual. the only consistency I noticed, apart from your playfully teasing voice, was pe you made sure our bodies connected, a cuddling, a hand-holding, or a prolonged hug, before saying it.

"let's commit suicide."

I have fallen in love with that sentence. the sublime confidence of it all. it's also funny. it's really funny tori pe it's you I should have fallen in love with. instead, it has become a personalized mantra. and my nightmare.

3.

death.

I want you to remember couples that have met God half-way. couples in real life o. not Romeo and Juliet, please. those guys are too stupid for serious attention. perhaps Jack and Rose (although Jack and Rose are still stupid and your ass can't even argue it with me this time). I'm asking you to remember couples that we may not personally know, sugbon whose stories transcend the compromise of fiction. love stories are not meant to be read or experienced in a chasm. there is more to them than meets the eye. ati pe no one can effectively capture all of it in writing.

I'm sorry. I'm rambling again. (was this why you slept with your neighbor, because I waste a lot of time and delay things? I feel it. I know you slept with him.)

I was starting to talk about people that decided—and succeeded—to die together.

you know I'm studying anthropology in school, right?

sorry for asking the obvious. there is so much I fear you would not remember, so much I fear you would rather remember.

Richard Horne, sixty-eight, encumbered by a terminal lung cancer, and his wife, Jean-Wright, seventy-two, winded by hepatitis, lay on their bed in America, inhaled toxic gas and left the world hands-locked. I bet you didn't know.

Charlie, eighty-eight, badly weakened heart, and Frankie Emerick, eighty-seven, prostate cancer, Parkinson's, took lethal doses of medication obtained under some Death With Dignity law, and died with joy.

ha. wait. you've not heard anything.

the saga in Egypt. the Irish woman and her Egyptian husband. they woke up one fine day and, nitori pe they had always been seeking to discover the other world, to know what happens after death, they wore their diving suits, wrapped heavy chains used in weight lifting around their necks, went to the Red Sea coast, into a villa in Hurghada, and drowned themselves in the swimming pool there.

and cetera. and cetera.

now... you and I... kani pe I agree to what you finally approved of my nonsense... tori pe it is nonsense to choose death when somebody wants to give you life for free... kani pe we want to be another headlines couple, how do we go about ours? how do we die? lethal doses? toxic inhalation? drowning?

or, for the sake of humor, do we go the standard way of the old joke, nibi ti we decide to jump off a cliff, and seconds after you jump, I am still standing on the edge? nigba ti I look down, a parachute is billowing right above your head and you are nodding to a safe landing. is that what we shall do? will betrayal enter our "surprise journey to God" pact, too? or, as has been argued, will we call it "last-moment fright"? are there even any rocks here in Sagamu? Sagamu may have that antique glory, hold a musty history so preciously, so gently, in its very air; heck, your scrappy little town may be charming in its insularity and lush with ambition, but perhaps we can now finally agree that it has nothing as beautiful as those rocks in Abeokuta.

how will we die, sweetheart?

4.

do you still want to do this?

are you guilty?

what's the point nigba ti, in six days, we will no longer be together?

you have convinced me that it's best we break up, yes, because you are pissed I don't trust you, yes, sugbon—why choose Valentine's day?

all those people I mentioned above, check their ages. they died as old people. they made sure they had enjoyed and suffered and survived together k'otodipe they took their lives. they fulfilled their love in death.

sugbon we... have we even begun our love? Emeka, have we even stayed half a decade together? nigbawo l'a meet, nigbawo ni our hearts bind unto each other? if your father didn't get transferred to Ogun state and if my uncle and aunt had not migrated to Abeokuta, would we have met at that fundraising in Sagamu? we might, anyway, but not in that way that made it seem like our stars aligned. we are young and we are fucked. if you want to argue, o ya, let's do it.

I know the case you'll bring up.

Mari and Mercedes. the teenage lovers who died. it is one of the most recent and the most salient. quite touching. sugbon they are just as young, and just as fucked. another thing is pe, unlike the aforementioned cases, they didn't die together. they died days apart. Mercedes took her life on the twentieth. Mari on twenty-second. both in an April that was as dark as this February.

I don't understand. are surprise journeys to God configured to happen in under-numbered months? April. February. is there something unforgivable, unmendable, about fuckups that happen in months that don't run up to thirty-one? February—is it an April Fool gone sour?

I don't understand. I want you to help me understand. at the same time, I don't want you to. tori pe you are running the same tracks. you use my words against me. you tell me too often that we should die together, inside the same cocoon that steamed us into this thickness.

why?

why?

5.

I understand self-harm. my wrists are reticulated libraries of slashed tales. you have always held them. you must have peered closely enough and seen the lacerations, tiny crisscross of razor that archived my first heartbreak. just after I left secondary school.

you must have noticed—you just never asked why.

I have done a lot more to myself. I have once held my forearm to my mouth and bitten hard. I have once stuffed pepper into my eyes and when my tears came, they came red and I collected them in a bowl from which I later used them to scrub my legs, hands, and penis. the same penis you fondled in the shadows of the palms between our dormitories nigba ti we were on campus. I'm still surprised by how quickly it healed, how stubbornly. oh, the resilience of our sexuality.

[long pause]

I also understand the need to startle God. I even want it.

last week, I attended church with my roommate. are you going to gasp nigba ti you hear that? where I sat, bi the organist was playing the hymn, I saw a mighty creature float up on gold-white wings. I pinched my arm to check, sugbon I was not asleep. I was not dreaming. more descended, humongous winged specters, their robes flowing without end, their feet not touching the linoleum of the church floor. they came away from the stained-glass window, away from the carved idols, away from the large Crucifix on the altar, and hover above the heads of the people. I could see through their feet, their bodies; they were like flying glass. they had no intestines, no hearts, just a permanent glow. I nudged my roommate to tell him, amo he was engrossed in the strains of the refrain. I looked in helplessness towards the congregation; none seemed to see what I saw. nigba ti service ended and we went home, I told roomie about it. I said to him, "I saw angels." he laughed and laughed and

40

pushed me outside. that night, I glared at the curtains at the door, waiting for the cherubs to come back, because I knew they would. but it was my roomie who startled me. he shot up from his bed. his eyes were stars and, in a voice that did not belong to him, he told me to go ahead and do it. "are you sure?" I asked him. sugbon he had plopped back into the bed and continued snoring. I asked him again the next morning and he said pe he knew nothing about the nonsense I was saying. then he waved me out of the way again.

from that day, I knew then: this is what I must do. the apparitions from God have brought the message. if they are angels of death, I do not know. sugbon, whatever they are, I don't want you to be in my plan. why? what would make you hate life so? you that are a teenager. we that are teenagers. you have your life rolled out brightly in front of you, like a red carpet. in fact, this would be your first serious breakup... your first heartbreak, I dare say. and no, I repeat: I am not leaving you, leaving everything, tori pe you slept with someone else. you love me, that's what I know; that's what matters. but don't enter bus on the same day I want to enter bus.

we are better off without each other. we don't have the strength to claim each other; we never did. so leave the dying to us that have been burned twice, because we have crayoned beauty into the flames and it calls out to us.

we don't have to become another Mari and Mercedes. they always told each other how they hated life and everything in it. Mari always tried to talk Mercedes out of it. sugbon she was stuck in it already. let it stay that way, my love. leave the leaving to me. at least I was the one who started the thought. leave it to me. don't come. they were like we are, even if their love was publicly approved. they were like we are; we mustn't be like they are.

this is all my fault, isn't it? I wouldn't shut up. I was always attacking people like you on Facebook, saying you are going against the will of God and twisting the Bible to suit "your" perversions and addictions. I called the sweat that dappled our connected bodies after we made love "perversions and addictions". I called your singing to me while you strummed your tacky red guitar "perversions and addictions". I called your dreams to have four kids with me and give them only-Yoruba names "perversions and addictions". they were never my dreams; I just watched you live them in your head, your eyes misting over, tori pe you assumed I was there in your head, living them with you. you would spoon-feed me and say, "Osita, are you sure we are not the weirdest Igbo people on earth?" and I would clench my jaw around the food, delaying my chewing, because chewing meant I would swallow and swallowing meant I could accidentally swallow the idea, the idea of giving only-Yoruba names to our children. children who wouldn't exist anyway.

you would call me "the proper Igbo boy", the one untainted by non-Igbo customs, and I would remind you of Owerri, the glittering openness of a city choked with versions of you and me. and you would laugh that eloquent laugh I still can't drown out of my head, no matter how much I drink. most times, though, if you remember, I didn't say anything. I would just smile and smile, because I knew what would happen if I didn't smile and remain silent. like that night in your room—it was raining heavily and the lamp was turned to its brightest and we were sitting on the carpet and licking ube and scraping roast corn with our teeth, and you said you missed Enugu, that you went through hell just to get the ube because I had told you I wanted them, and I smiled and said nothing. I actually wanted to say that you shouldn't have bothered. sibe, no matter how hard I tried, I couldn't hold my poison in my stomach without passing it to you.

the first time I talked to you nipa suicide, your eyes had popped open and you had asked me not to mention it again. then, the following week, while we were in your backyard, washing your jeans and T-shirts, you looked at me for so long that I began to squirm and you said you had been thinking seriously about suicide. you said happy people don't commit suicide. pe if that was what would make us happy, then we should do it. and I gaped at you, unable to find words, while the lather dried on my hands, nitori pe this was bigger than words for me... then I finally asked, "but we are happy, are we not?"

and you laughed.

6.

happiness—how is it defined? our lecturer once asked us in an assignment to write about *The Happiness of Successful People*. what is happiness generally? is it a state of not having lost anyone in your family, either to death or to divorce or to separation?

is it happiness nigba ti we are excelling at our academics? you know I failed to mention the students we lost last year alone in OOU? that Part 4 Political Science student whose door had to be broken down tori pe it was locked from behind, before they could find him in his mattress, decaying, a Sniper bottle lying next to him. and a note that nobody should cry for him.

what about the Law student who said they must bury him with his law books and rosary, or else, his ghost would come back and haunt everyone on campus, starting from his hostel block?

is happiness self-confidence, is it a healthy self-esteem? are we happy nigba ti our friends are still interested in us and we are still interested in them? are we happy nigba ti we can enjoy hobbies, or anticipate activities previously enjoyed?

is happiness even defined or simply felt, or held tightly?

I want to know what it is all about.

is happiness the lack of sadness? is it nigba ti we are not sad, withdrawn, apathetic? is it nigba ti when we are not irritable? is it the lack of anxiety? the absence of nightmares from our eyes and hearts? is it nigba ti we are not tired, nigba ti we can concentrate on routine tasks like school and work?

I don't think so. it can't just be that simple. abi why would someone post a so-full-of-life picture of him and his girlfriend smiling and skating on Instagram yesterday, and today, the news brings it that they have drunk something that tore their intestines to molded shreds?

and why would we *crave* to die, we two teenagers just ripening in university?

are we self-absorbed, building an obsessive pity shrine for ourselves that we must always honor with people's sympathies?

are we overwhelmed—by guilt, shame, self-hatred?

if happiness is the presence of dreams in our eyes and hearts, if happiness means we can still sleep normally, no unders, no overs, if we can still eat without losing or gaining pounds we don't plan for, then why do I find it queer to be happy? and how do you just wake up and finally *agree* to die?

I thought you were happy. I thought you dreamed other dreams.

[another explosive sneeze]

oh my God…

[pause again—longer than the first, then the sound of sniffing, not just nasal, like tears]

why is it happening like this? I'm running mad here. I need to know.

why is it happening like this? has something happened to my organs? why am I in so much body pain? am I dying alive?

I would go to the clinic; sugbon what if they stare and point at me, or leave the road when I'm passing?

it would be easier kani pe you were here. you would at least be with me. I will hide under your strong shoulder. I don't even want to leave this room.

[more sound of crying]

I'm scared, Emeka. I'm so scared. am I just a dreamer—and nothing more? there was a time I would think I am also lying to myself. there are tons of my messages that you left unread, even bi your status story still doesn't rest with pictures of strange people that you caption with the love emoji, pictures you insist I shouldn't read meaning into.

but that time is gone. I *know* you love me. that you even want to do this with me proves it.

but why?

is it fear for me? a seething, self-loathing, deep-seated fear?

of what? skydiving? losing control? hitting rocks? of things ending inevitably?

do we go to death because we don't want to die?

what is it for *you*?

are you convinced the future you dreamed will never come? pe things will never get better? pe nothing will ever change? pe I will never forgive you for what you did—nor forget?

is that what makes us die?

7.

sweetheart, fucking answer me!

[pause, very short]

8.

oh sorry, I forgot this is a voicenote, and pe by the time you would reply this, I will be long gone.

the blood is not just in my nostrils, not just on my hands. I keep seeing it in my dreams, too. a red endlessness. my soul cut away from the world. blood and feathers stuck in it. and then more blood, for the day that Osita Ukwueze died. and that bottle with you gazing at me, for the day you—the day you what? I don't get it. it's bizarre. macabre. I don't fucking understand.

I see a coiled rope dangling from the ceiling. a dusty old scarf tied to a still fan-blade. I should understand all of that. I see a big shiny knife, held by someone, nothing on it, and then I see the bottle with your head on it. your head in my dream does not have misty eyes. your head in my dream is mottled with heart-shapes.

your mantra, "let's commit suicide"—even in its scuffed ordinariness—has become like some grand eerie music. I tap-dance to it in my sleep.

[laughter]

I sleep naked.

it is a personal rite.

it is my prayer to you.

to think not, when you send me on this journey, of joining me.

you will send me alone. then you will let me go alone.

that way I may be happy wherever I am. and at least you *will* be happy.

I am the cloud that has eclipsed your sunshine.

now that my madness has increased… I am imagining your reaction.

let me hear you listen.

eh? you said?

did you mention hell fire? God's wrath?

[loud laughter]

it feels like hell *already*. it feels like God's wrath. I can't love. I can't breathe. it hurts to inhale and exhale. I can't place you in my heart. I can't give joy to you who tried to give me. tell me again what hell feels like.

I have chosen to do this on my own, for us.

47

I had been waiting before, but now there's no more need to wait.

six more days, and all this will be over.

they will be over.

and then, sweetheart, you can live your life.

and find love again—if it's your destiny, whether it's your neighbor or not.

[long pause]

I wish you were here. I want to lay my head on your shoulder. this so-called iba is so hot in my body...

I have a low battery. I have to send this eighth one, or else you won't know anything at all. the next voice of me ti you will hear will be in your dream, if you dream, Emeka obi m.

[*kpikim]

BAR BOY

At first, their story seemed to begin—to him—like a sticky memory wiped across a flat surface. Later, when Shina would tell it to his friends at a sports club party, he would say it eventually became like sitting in front of a mammoth screen and having someone play you the déjà vu reel of your life. Only that this time, they let you pause the motions and make different decisions for yourself. He would tell it laughing, his cheeks rumpled with gratitude. But that evening, his face was frozen in awe as the boy spoke.

"But people are mad *sha*! Why would you gather thugs to go and beat your brother's wife in the middle of the street! Who does that and goes like a bird? In this twenty-first century, *hunnay*. Palpable bushness!"

Shina made a wry face; he loved the sharp way with which the phrase *palpable bushness* had burst out of the boy's mouth. He smiled and said, "I agree it's a barbaric act."

"Very!"

The boy raised his tall cup to his lips, the thirteenth time now in Shina's calculation. He could not be more than eighteen years' old. If there was any alteration to that deduction, then he would be seventeen, or even sixteen. And here he was, guzzling red wine as if it were a *zobo* drink! Shina was almost gaping. He wondered if it was all a coping mechanism. The table was emptying, both of people and of food and drinks. It had been a helluva fun night: drag runs,

49

Voguing, tequila contests, Truth or Dare. Shina stared at the tables: perfect shrimps curled inside clear bowls, piping-hot pepper soup, cocktail with their tiny rainbow umbrellas, crumbly croissants, shish kebabs, ultra-thin spaghetti bolognese, chicken drenched in orange sauce, cold sparkling Chardonnay, loosely dressed young men and women talking loudly and eating loudly and laughing loudly, with or without their partners, as if to overappreciate an avenue to finally dare to live noisily. One of the anchors wore an off-shoulder cocktail ensemble, profuse in feathers and sequins, with ripped tights and a leather mini that left swathes of muscles screaming up and down their legs. Their wig was greased and singed straight. Their face and feet were a pandemonium of colors: their eyelids drenched in purple glitters, a luridly unsettling gash of red on their lips, a crimson clutch in their elbow and a flashy pair of green Rihanna-thin stilettos stabbing the tiles. For an insufferably long while, the costume became the major at many tables. Someone shouted, "Go, RuPaul's A-list queen!" and that elicited more laughter than it should. Nobody mentioned the conspicuous absence of breasts and hips that might be too exaggerated for a nonbinary transvestite to exhibit. But this anchor wouldn't have cared; they strutted across the floors, ruling their world. It was all good cheer. No space in the air for bitter jibes. It was a grand-finale dinner party hosted by a Sexual Minorities Issues organization, come all the way from Lagos, in honor of people living with HIV/AIDS. And Shina didn't know what the hell he was doing there. Except for the fact that he was gawking at the mouth of this frail-looking, too-young boy who raised his glass and swigged.

"Like, Mecca, the man fucked up, though!" protested Savage Gold. He was the one who had told the current story of how a man in Port Harcourt had hired thugs to beat up his own sister-in-law. The woman was found guilty of suing his brother when she found out he was actually gay and lying. Savage Gold was chubby, and upset that his point had been missed. He had seven gold teeth and an interesting way of putting "Mecca" in all his sentences.

"Yes, he did," the boy said. "Why would you go and lie to everyone in the first place? Why would you deliberately marry someone you could not be true to?"

"Mecca!" Savage Gold rejoiced. "You're finally getting my point."

"It's the 'Tb' mentality," Shina said, slowly sipping his Smirnoff. "Everybody expects gay men to marry women, and gay men also expect to marry women. So they marry women and come back into the streets to chase boys."

"They are dissatisfied! Mecca, I could never go that low. That's just a painful thing to go through!" Savage Gold wailed, wringing his hands; there was a gold ring on each of those ten fingers; they were blinding in the lights.

The boy inspected his glass carefully before speaking. "I hate the way we make this sound like it's an inevitable end for a gay man. There is nothing greedy or helpless about these MGMs. They knew exactly what they were walking into, and they walked into it, eyes wide open. They were just self-neglecting and self-hating. Same thing goes for many bisexual men who find enduring love with a man, but still opt to marry a woman and then say, 'It's because it's Nigeria, and for my parents, too.' They know they wouldn't leave their male loves alone even after their marriage. Nobody dragged them into society marriage. I repeat: they were just being self-abandoning."

There was a series of "Well, well, well, the actual pointers, boy be making sense right there", heads bobbing around the table, people swishing wine around in their cheeks thoughtfully. But Shina still spoke, risking everything. He was familiar with people like the boy—they were opinionated hotheads.

"Sometimes, though," he leaned forward and clasped his hands, "these men do it out of choicelessness. It's the bloody society. We have many hypertensive parents out there and nobody wants to be the reason a parent died on them."

"So they choose to be the ones to die instead by living in sad and unfaithful companionships? How noble!" The boy shook his head as though Shina was already a lost cause.

Shina swallowed. Navigating the waters of biphobia in the community had always been tricky. He was used to people getting excited with him during the talking stage in his DMs, and fading out with just as much energy when he told them he had once been married to a woman. He thought that it was righteous of them, unforgivingly judgmental, but he also wondered what he would do, were he in their shoes. So he swallowed it. He swallowed, also, the story of his bicurious friend, Hakeem, who had kids with a woman, found love with a man, and came out to his wife. She wouldn't let him leave, so he had an affair with the man and she of course found out and put him under so much pressure that he hanged himself.

"I agree," said Ifejirika, a gangling man who had made everyone giggle the previous night when he walked up to the podium in a pair of three-quarters and nothing else to share his Positive Story. "How can I choose what my parents want again? I have been choosing what they want all my life. When will I start choosing my own wants, especially in a serious thing like marriage?"

"*Gworl.* God bless you *o!*" the boy said, spreading out his palms, rolling his eyes to the vaulted ceiling.

Shina wanted to laugh, to grab that long neck and drive kisses into it and laugh and laugh and laugh. "Well," he said, trying not to sound too somber so his own story would not seep out, "marriage is serious, and it's the reason I'm still single."

The boy shot him a glance.

"Marrying a woman as a gay man is the most foolish thing ever! That is why their poor, unloved wives get stopped in their cars—Mecca!—on a deserted road and get beaten up by thugs!" Savage Gold yelped, determined to drag the conversation back to his own agitation.

"Yeah. A foolish move, but also a Marlian move," Shina quipped, and the boy flashed him another quick, intrigued look. Shina tried to wink, but the boy's eyes had gone, disinterest replacing intensity so swiftly, so dramatically, that Shina wondered if he had imagined things.

He looked round the table, people living with HIV and people who wanted to know if they could live with people who lived with HIV, and he wondered again where he belonged. Surely not with the people who wanted to know how to live with reactive people, because he was a virologist and a private medical doctor and so he knew how to live, and even sleep, with reactive people. And surely, neither did he belong with the silly quack specialists who had met them at the entrance of the Abuja hotel hall two days ago when the programme kicked off, carrying the necessary cardboard enlightenments—*HIV IS* NOT *A CURSE FROM GOD! IT'S TREACHEROUS, DON'T HIDE IT! YOU CAN LIVE AS NORMALLY AS NON-REACTIVE FOLKS DO! THIS IS THE BEST TIME TO BE ALIVE!*—but also offering attendants the more pernicious information that only the ARVs and HAARTs in their hands could flush out their viral load. Fortunately, the organizers had passed a law that nobody should sell or buy anything inside or outside the hotel, except from the specialists whose names and pictures were placed in the pamphlets the ushers had distributed. Shina had been able to convince some of the attendants that, even though the organizers recognized the specialists in the pamphlets, it was still highly possible to have scam trade happen. "Be careful, too many hungry people and too many fake drugs out there," he had said to the people he had been able to walk to and talk to. Among the ones who had seemed ready to listen to him were Ifejirika, Savage Gold and the boy. That was the reason he had chosen their table for the dinner, he told himself, it wasn't because of the boy's soft-looking red lips.

"But really," Ifejirika wanted to be sure, "is it cowardice that makes gay men marry women? Or just plain wickedness. Especially many bisexual men who know in their heart of hearts o that it's a man they would love to marry o. They will now marry finish and be disturbing us! *Ndi apari!*"

The boy and Savage Gold cackled cheerily. It had always been a juicy pastime, destroying bisexuals.

"Sorry, hunnay," the boy said, his tone lined with sarcasm, a mocking consolation in his beady, kohl-rimmed eyes. "The balances of the world have been unfairly placed."

"Somebody has got to start fixing those bloody balances, *maka Chukwu*!" Ifejirika raged. "*This life no balance. This life no balance.* What about you—you balance so?"

"Mad ooo!" the boy and Savage Gold chorused and dissolved into guffaws.

"Guys, we live in a place where we are asked and trained to behave like that," Shina chipped in, assured that he sounded intelligent. "We make certain life choices to let peace reign and to take eyes off our lives. Fuck what we really want."

But the boy wailed, "That's a lot of hogwash! Nobody with a sense of dignity can be made to do what they don't want to do. I insist! It is self-neglect that makes people opt for what they would rather not do. That's not society's problem. That's the individual's problem."

"*Purrr, bae*, I agree to that one," said Ifejirika, grateful to have finally found a supporter. "It is never society's problem. I know one boy who came out to his parents while he was living with them. And both of them are conservative old-testamental pastors. Imagine that!" Then he turned to Shina, his long dangling arms propped on the table. "And what's with the defense, mister? Are you an MGM?"

Shina, smarting under the pepper-hot rejoinders, could only gawk. Savage Gold came to the rescue.

"Mecca. How can you exonerate society, when people are cowardly only because of the threat of society?"

Iferijika looked at the boy. The boy merely laughed as if Shina and Savage Gold didn't really know what they were saying, and raised the cup to his lips again.

•••

Shina wanted to kiss those lips. They were red and looked delicious enough for thirty days of sin. But he must slap them first! What nonsense! How rude of the boy. Heck, he—Shina—must be at least fifteen years older than him. Running his mouth like that! Shina was appalled. He imagined the boy on Facebook. He would be insolent and incandescent and hated and loved.

And they were *wrong*. He was not an MGM; he was an MQM, a bicurious man who married a woman. He divorced his wife, miraculously amicably, just this past December. She had initiated it, a little too quickly for a woman who was supposed to be a heartbroken wife. Good riddance; he had always thought she was a closeted lesbian anyway. They had twins, and it was agreed that each parent should take one child into custody. He didn't know exactly how he felt— whether like a bird finally released from a cage or like a bird moved from one cage into another—but he sure did feel sorry for his two boys. How telling, what the state of a marriage could do to the children brought into it. Already, the son living with his wife was being suspended serially for jumping class and beating up his classmates, things he had never for once done when the family was still patched together. One more act of delinquency and he would be kicked out. Shina thought he should start going about how to appeal that he take the second son into his custody, too. A lumpy stone sat in his soul. You gave your whole life to a place, and then turned around only to realize it was the wrong place.

"Ahn ahn, Dr Shina!"

He jolted back to the table. The three of them were peering at him quizzically.

"What were you thinking about?" Ifejirika asked.

"Uh, nothing serious."

"*Chile!* I hope it wasn't a clapback o," the boy said. "'Cause that would be an awfully protracted time to give a clapback."

Shina chuckled, surprised at how easily the sounds left his throat. "No, I wouldn't give a clapback. I'm too old for a clapback."

"Says who? You're still damn cute." Ifejirika sidled up with his long hands.

"Mecca! Somebody's shooting shots!" Savage Gold had on a silly, corrupt grin.

The boy said, "Durrh", and rolled his eyes. "You're just a hoe."

Ifejirika gasped. "I'm not!"

"Mecca, you are."

"It's the thirst for me," the boy murmured.

"Like, what are you two onto?" Ifejirika was histrionically incredulous. He spread out his hands and gawped. "This man is hot as *fuck*. *Look* at him. He looks like a boy!"

"We know!" the boy snapped.

"That shiny dark skin alone. The ebony is out of this world." Ifejirika could have been licking *oha* soup off its ladle. He looked so starry-eyed.

"Eat him then," the boy said.

"Allah have mercy. Oluwa wetin dey cannibalate? Mecca!"

"He already unbuttoned his shirt halfway. He doesn't look like he would mind being eaten."

Shina wanted to laugh hard, instead of the cultured chuckles jerking his shoulders, but he was too self-conscious around the boy. He liked their effervescence, their ability to be ballsy and buoyant. Ifejirika, especially, who had narrated the story of his ex, how the man—an exporter of rubber in Delta—would lock him up for days, beating and raping him, because news on the vine said Ifejirika was a serial cheat, and so had to be "monitored". "He monitored me with enough slaps and kicks to blind me," Ifejirika had said. "But who was I to complain to— that what? That a man is beating another man because they are fucking? Who will hear that one? I simply started drugging him and then, one afternoon while he was in his plantation, I took his money and fled. Yes o! I think all the oil crises his homeland suffers combined to make him an internally disturbed person. It was not me he would kill with national vex o." Despite the graveness of the moment, there had been laughter. Only the boy's disposition appeared crusted with rough edges, carrying his reservations, a knowledge that came with a burden, as though what he thought mattered more than what they laughed at.

Shina looked on now as they traded what they called "readings" among themselves over his looks. He was used to people interjecting, during Facebook or WhatsApp chats, that he "sounded" young—sending top-accurate stickers, using colloquialisms like "Shawty" and "BDSM kee you dia"—and yet when he sent them a picture of himself on selected demand, they started doubting that he was really the one. How could a forty-one-year-old man look so youthful, so perfectly chiseled? And he would laugh and tell them it was one of the reasons he didn't keep a visible profile on Facebook and had no DP on his WhatsApp, because if he did, he might not be able to read and focus on his PhD in this life. It was familiar then, this evening, to thoroughly enjoy the attention from the three young men. He watched them banter about him for a while before speaking. "But you people too are cute *na*!"

The boy made a gagged face. Savage Gold picked up his glass and rolled his eyes. Ifejirika burst into tears. "It's a lie! Don't lie!", and then he went on to tell the story of the corper who wanted to hook up with him in Ilorin, and when Ifejirika finally plucked up the courage and went to the guy's self-contained lodge, he opened the door and told Ifejirika that Ifejirika was too ugly to be gay. And be a Bottom-roler at that, too. And what the hell was that filter he used on his online pictures anyway? It was enough to get anyone arrested.

"Mecca! The burn of it all."

"*Gworl*. But you have suffered at the hands of men sha," the boy said. "Only you? *God abeg*."

Everybody laughed, including Ifejirika himself, cleaning off his tiny tears.

"Look at you. Waka-waka. All the way to Ilorin. Mecca! Be thankful you were not Kitoed!" Savage Gold said.

"I was so shocked I couldn't find the door anymore."

"*Eeyah*," said the boy, raising glass to lips. "You have seen *shege banza*."

"Oh, is that the one you heard?" Savage Gold said. "One said I was too handsome to be gay. That hundreds of women had lost their potential husband. I said, 'Mecca!' "

Ifejirika and Shina chortled.

59

"But how can you lose something that was never yours to begin with? Has it ever been certain that even if you were heterosexual, you would automatically be interested in these women?" the boy asked.

"I wonder," Shina said, suddenly steeped in epiphanies. He shouldn't have had that wedding. He had felt like weeping in church that Saturday morning as the pastor joined two people that did not agree and would never agree to walk together. He had only gone ahead with it, spent those years with her, to convince himself.

"This is why homophobia is dangerous, more so for heterosexual people, because homophobia drives people into closets and clueless folks end up marrying these closeted gay people. It's really a vicious circle," said the boy.

There was another general nod of agreement.

"But—to be fair—we still see women doing everything they can to get ungettable guys," Shina said. "My, er, my colleague's wife chased him and chased him. But man wouldn't be straight even if they plastered him into a church pillar."

The table shook. There were shouts of "*preeeach!*" replete with whistles.

"Oh, I thought that was a man's thing, the whole chasing thing," Savage Gold said, fork-poking the curried lamb.

"Don't be silly," the boy reprimanded. "Desperation and its expressions know no gender. There is always something about the unavailable that makes it even more desirable."

"Hmm, that's deep," said Shina with exaggerated fervor, but the boy merely spared him a dull glance, his expression arch and adrift. Fleetingly, Shina wondered if the boy perhaps did drugs, serious hard drugs.

"That's true sha," Ifejirika said. "When someone is hard to get, everybody behaves as if they are under siege. I heard of a lady in my hometown who couldn't successfully seduce her aunt's husband and so she went to a *dibia* for serious powder to put in his pepper!"

"Did it work?" Savage Gold asked.

"*Pfft*," the boy sneered, staring with genuine horror at Savage Gold as if he honestly could not believe anyone would possibly be interested in Ifejirika's newest story.

"Who knows? People said it worked. That the man gave her *belle* and threw her aunt's bags outside in the rain."

"Mecca! I think I have the full video!" Savage Gold said.

"But really, why do people go to all that trouble for something that can never last?" Ifejirika asked.

"Na them sabi ooo, Mecca. Las las, the person go wise up and curve them. Brutal curving o!"

"*O di egwu*. They hear and read stories of these woeful endings on Instablog9ja o, sometimes even resulting in death, but they keep on doing it."

"Will they hear? Na their type dey do 'hide my ID, admin'. Suffering done master them. Mecca ooo. Dem go tell you say life na ocean; say na fish chop fish o."

"Why do we say stuff like 'suffering done master them' when it is we that actually master *in* suffering?" the boy said.

He had on that same hooded gaze, like someone high on psychedelic substances.

"Oh, Mecca, come on, it's not that deep! It's just pidgin!" Savage Gold rolled his eyes and flipped an imaginary wig.

"I see."

Savage Gold unlocked his phone and started typing furiously. Ifejirika concentrated on his orange chicken. Shina stared. There was something about the boy, a questioningness, bracing and building, that made Shina want to be more intelligent.

The boy spoke again. "It's just like when I was in Ebonyi and a boy wrote in his exercise book that 'they were laughing me'. I was too appalled to hold the pen straight."

"*Chile*, *sisturr*, you and straight don't match." Savage Gold looked up from his phone and giggled. "Mecca!"

The boy raised his glass and winked. "You bet."

Shina asked, "When did this happen?"

"When I was teaching. I taught before gaining admission into university."

Shina paused. "How old are you?"

"Nineteen."

Oh, okay, he was wrong. But wasn't far from right. He longed to know more.

"What's your name, please?"

The boy took his time studying his emptied glass as though it were alien apparatus before saying, "Oye."

"What does it mean? Is it Yoruba?"

"Yes."

"Oh... You're Yoruba."

The boy laughed, refilled his cup and raised it again. "What did you think I was? A European?"

Oye roared into the night. Shina was tongue-tied.

•••

When he first met them, it was the second day of the programme. It was tagged: Positive Story Hear-Out Evening. Everyone who wanted to would have the opportunity to share the story of learning about their reactive status, how far they had come, how far they still had to go, and how much the journey had compressed and severed the relationships in their lives. Some of the stories had amused him. The first speaker said his name was Gospel and that he was from Benue. "Well, as you all know my people are already known for HIV, so everybody just assumed stuff about my status. Till tomorrow, they still think I got it from a woman o, and I think of it as a sordid kind of justice," he had said into the mike and people had managed not to snicker. But they laughed noisily when a young man said, with a thick rural Igbo accent, after a tirade about his parents' insistence on taking him to a Catholic priest and performing extreme unction on him to drive out the spirits of HIV and homosexuality, "This bottle line has just been drawn."

Shoulders shook.

"He was just trying too hard to show us all that he could speak English," the man seated next to Shina leaned sideways to say, in a strong Hausa accent and a stronger whiff of tobacco.

63

"Apparently, he wasn't trying to stop you from showing your own English," Oye, sitting directly in front of Shina, had looked back to say. And Shina had studied him—the boy was easily the youngest in that room—and been charmed by the unassailable irreverence of teenage, and how easily it could be forgiven.

Several more people had walked up to the podium to speak their courage, tragedies and fears into the small portable mike. But it was the boy's story, delivered in a drab, offhand, almost insouciant manner, that had held Shina's heart.

"I was raped at a stupid birthday party in Maitama. Five men. They didn't wear anything. It was my deflowering. Knowing about my status gave me the boldness to come out to my family. I came out to my younger brother first. I was startled at the way he cut me short and said he had always known and that as long as I didn't bring 'that shit' near him, we good." He cracked off a mirthless laughter that had broken Shina's heart into small pieces. "They are praying for me," Oye continued, and then stopped talking.

A silence had fallen on the room, a funereal, cumbersome cloud, and Shina had loathed the fact that everyone was mourning Oye, who was not mourning himself. When he spoke again, people were aghast that his voice was still level.

"My mum tried to handle it. She bought me my early ARVs. Please help me clap for that woman. My dad was the fiercest against the situation. He said I was being punished. That I am positive because I am gay. I laughed so hard. Isn't it funny, how people approve of our illnesses when they believe illnesses are our portions for what we did or what we are? I told him I was positive long before I knew what sleeping with someone was. Everybody told me I was the accursed of God. But they didn't tell me the things I could be, the things that I actually was. Nobody told us the things they tell their straight kids. Me? Nobody told me I could have self-worth. That I could listen to my body and respect it a little more. I need to stop talking, like, right now. I need a smoke."

Shina was frozen in his seat. He watched Oye disappear through a side door. He remained in his seat but barely heard the other speakers. Afterwards, he caught Oye in the hallway, drifted towards him and started expatiating on things he assumed might have been missed during the specialist awareness speech session.

"The next thing to realize after knowing that you can live your life happily after testing positive is that you must lower your corrupt CD4," he had said earnestly, worried that Oye would leave in a huff of impatience. "It will help lower your viral load. That man didn't add that. Only then can you begin to lower your antibodies AGGT, treat OIs and implications, and extract ISM bricks. After all that, you still have to raise your CD4 back to normal. I have the right prescriptions."

"Why should I believe you?" Oye snapped.

"Because I have the right prescriptions and you need to use them. And would you please try not to interrupt me because every time wasted counts. You have probably heard of all this before, but reiteration matters. The best ways to remove viral load are blood sterilization and nanorobotics. You can also use oxygenated saline, silver, zinc, sulphaminoglycans. All these will be intravenously administered. You can tell mummy that you will be fine.

65

You will also use Ciclopirox drugs. Don't worry; I'll text you all the details so you can go over them."

The boy narrowed his eyes. "How will you text me the details when you don't have my number? Oh! Is that the new format? Not so *smooov* if you ask me."

Shina scratched his head. "See. All those ARVs and HAARTs some of them were talking about are just to suppress the viral load. They can't prevent aggressive hyperfulminant infections. Did you hear?"

"Okay! I've heard! Jesus Christ! Can I go back to my room now?"

"What's your room number?" Shina asked; barriers had been broken by Oye's waiting, and now blitheness could germinate through the open spaces.

"207."

And Shina had grinned from ear to ear, his first smile that afternoon.

•••

Savage Gold was still punching his phone. The ushers were passing a list around for everyone to drop their contacts for a follow-up WhatsApp group to be created for the attendees. But when it got to their table and everyone, even Shina, wrote down their number and passed it to Oye, Oye passed it to the next table without writing. His tablemates said nothing, only looked at him askance, as if he had just committed a most infamous act. As they retired each into their room for the night in preparation for tomorrow's journey back to their respective origins, Shina drifted to Oye again. Stopped at the door. And knocked, gingerly.

"It's Dr Shina. May I enter?"

"Wait." There was a little rustling. "Okay, come right in."

He walked in, half expecting to meet Oye spread-eagled on the bed, masturbating with Goya Olive Oil.

"Make yourself comfortable. To what do I owe this visit?"

Shina ran his eyes all over Oye's naked back. He sat on the bed, surprised at his own audacity. "I'm curious about you."

"Curious?"

"Yes. I want to hear the part you didn't say back there, last night. I want to hear that part you chose to keep away."

Oye laughed. He was sitting at a vanity desk, peering into the clean mirror and rubbing a cream into his face. He was naked but for a pair of boyshorts. Shina felt himself harden.

"Come on. Is this about what I said about the man who was talking about his status and kept on saying 'the plague, the plague'?"

Shina was startled. "No...no. I didn't even remember it."

Oye kneaded his face. *How smooth it looks*, thought Shina, wanting to touch that skin.

"That man must have watched too many Billy Porter Pose scenes," Oye said and laughed again.

"Billy Porter is great," Shina said, a little caustically, because he liked the guy who had spoken—there was an innocence about him that he had liked—and he liked Billy Porter, too.

Oye turned slightly, his countenance surprised. "I didn't say Billy Porter wasn't great, sweetheart."

Shina felt the vertigo of the unexpectedly co-opted. That word "sweetheart" sounded like "welcome to heaven" from the boy's red lips. He laughed.

"When they passed that list round, why didn't you write your name?"

"Another WhatsApp group? Abeg!"

"This is not just 'another WhatsApp group', you know?"

"It's just another WhatsApp group, and I know. More flirting. More shading. More ego trips. More hookups. Please, avoid me. Whatever I want to know I will know. I have a doctor."

Shina felt a pang akin to loss. "You already have a doctor?"

"Yes. I have a support system. I have a doctor."

He should have guessed it. The bored expression on the boy's face back in the hall while he had rambled on to him about how to deal with his viral load should have indicated that Oye had a medical bank already. "Who?"

"He is sitting on my bed, worrying me."

And despite himself, Shina grinned like a child who took first position in a class of rivals.

Oye was looking from inside the mirror. "Ha, you are blushing."

"I don't even know what's wrong with me; guess I'm moonstruck."

"Moonstruck? Now that's serious. That would mean you're in love, eh?"

Shiba twiddled his fingers. "Would you be my Val?" His nervousness had pushed out those words.

"Wow. Just three days away. That's sweet. Nobody had ever asked me."

"That's a lie."

"That's the truth."

"No way! How come!"

"The first person I dated had an IH as big as Zuma Rock. Plus he couldn't handle that I have HIV, so we broke up before Valentine's Day would come and complicate things."

"Wawu."

"The second person I went out with did not ask me to be his Val. He just took me. And then we got there and he picked up his phone and started inviting his friends to join us. We broke up the day after."

"Okay, that's another level of Marlianism shit." Shina was laughing, freeing all the buttons inside him, no longer feeling sorry for his estranged kids. They would have a new father soon. A crazy, young, Marlian father with red lips. He was full of brightly colored dreams.

"And the last person I dated, that was 2018, was a Deeper Life member."

"Oh, I know the story!"

They were both chuckling. And Shina felt taken, irredeemably, by the magical mixture of the familiar and the funny.

"Look at your hard-on." Oye was pointing.

Shina looked down; he had convinced himself that the pressure flexing against his inner thigh was his imagination. He was wrong.

"You're lucky I just cleaned up," Oye said, looking significantly in the direction of the bathroom.

Shina nodded slowly.

Then sparks became fire. They tumbled against the rumpled sheets, leaving a new tousling. They took each other's lips, like wild animals, sucking and pulling, chewing without teeth, until their mouths felt raw and oversoft. Oye ripped off Shina's shirt. Shina crouched over him, their groins grinding. With gentle bites, he burned holes into Oye's body, squeezing his buttocks. Oye quivered and spoke in other tongues. His left nipple swelled and tickled under Shina's tongue. He held Shina's head to his chest, felt it snake downward. His navel started goosefleshing under the tongue's pointed edge and he gave a soft cry. Shina tucked his fingers around the hem of Oye's boyshorts and rolled them down his thighs, down his ankles, and completely off. Oye's dick sprang into view like a mast. Shina wrapped his lips around it. He trailed his dripping tongue down the length, then started swiping slushily, swallowing the cap and popping it out back again, burying the shaft in his throat and sliding it out back through his lips, his eyes rolling up to hook Oye's. Oye spread his legs, threw his head back and moaned. When Shina's tongue reached the end of his balls, to the parting of his ass crack, he grabbed Shina's head and said a loud "Amen!" Shina almost burst out laughing. The walls were soundproof, but he wondered about how far the exclamation had traveled. Holding Oye's thighs spread open, he nosed into his crack

70

and savored the must with a drawn-out moan, then slid in his tongue, wetly, digging, lapping up, flicking it in and out, sucking and blowing on the flesh. Oye pulled at the pillows, restlessly. His legs shook. He could feel them no more. He propped them up Shina's shoulders. Shina gripped him and ate him up like well-creamed coleslaw. He shut his lips between Oye's ass cheeks and let his tongue do the wet center jiggling. When the trembling above his shoulders became frenzied, he leaned up, leaned over and lifted Oye off the bed, now locking lips with him. Oye was astride him, moving, straining, obviously desperate to feel all of him. Shina felt his hands on his body, groping to unbuckle the belt from his waist. He smiled. When Oye held him and brought him out, Shina bore him to the nearest windowsill, their chests fastened to each other. Oye held onto his turgid length and wouldn't let go. Soon, Shina's jeans were crumpled on the floor. He squeezed Oye's ass cheeks and Oye gripped him back in exquisite delight, rubbing the penis in his hand up and down the tender circumference of his bussy, stroking the shaft of the same penis. Shina gasped. He lengthened in Oye's hand. He reached over, slipped his middle finger between Oye's ass cheeks, found the entrance and slowly slid it in. Oye moaned into his mouth. A few more gentle thrusts with his finger, and Shina could feel the slippery coolness around his flesh already. He added a second finger and guided them in deeply until Oye's legs started trembling again. Scared that he would fall over from the window or smash a vase, Shina picked him up and carried him back to bed. There they lay on the cool sheets, naked and entwined, Oye's bussy wet and hungry and dripping while Shina slipped on a condom, rubbed it down the curved length and girth of his penis and gently pushed in, his mouth latched to Oye's. It was so renewing, his body remembering. His body waking up. He stroked his way in

71

rhythmically, as though he were doing a slow dance, whining his waist and grinding in deep, his lips patting circles around Oye's nipples, then his warm breath spreading across the pit of Oye's neck, crackling out fatal tremors. He took his time—he needed to savor this moment, this ritual of his true birth. Oye reached over and raked his nails down his back. Shina smiled, knowing that he was hitting the prostate. When he felt the creamy-cool moisture flow out and seep around his own dick, he confirmed that he was still in touch with his long-deep stroke game. He was still rocking the gates gently, prodding slowly, when Oye grabbed his butt and whispered fiercely, "Fuck me. Don't hesitate." That was the signal Shina had been waiting for—his butt gripped by Oye's hands. He picked up speed, a little speed, and Oye's moan became heightened gasps. Oye wrapped his legs around Shina's waist and refused to slacken them. They jerked back and forth, together, a locked mass of bodies.

Shina came four times. A tickling rush of fluids spurting out of his cap, repeatedly filling the condom, like egg syrup. Oye did not have to touch himself to come; he kept on spraying Shina's chest. At one point, he asked Shina to be still; then he turned over, fast-forwarded to his knees, widened the angle of his thighs and arched his back while Shina vibrated from behind. *Slap-slap-slap.* Sweat dropped on the bed. Oye almost forgot about his ARV dosage. But when it was time to come for the last time, Shina reminded him. Oye lay on his back afterward, his foot up on Shina's shoulder, watching Shina murmur gibberish. Shina's thrusts became pointed amnesties, begging for release. He slipped out, peeled off the strong condom, careful not to spill anything, took his dick in his own hand and went into heaven. His earlier youth, his dreams, his mistakes, his missed chances, his new chances—these were the things he thought of, just before he groaned throatily, finally, his muscles clenching, and smeared the boy's belly with his last precious, broken cum.

Oye could not walk to his bag to get the drugs. Shina had to help him, even though he himself was ungainly on his feet. He had never lost himself like that before in ethereal clouds; he had never ejaculated so much in his life.

•••

"What the hell did we just do?" he was asking, an hour and two baths later. They were in bed, cuddling.

"We fucked." Oye leaned further into his arms.

"Wow. You jazzed me." He wanted to bite Oye's ear, softly, with his lips.

"Oh please." Oye rolled his eyes. "If I did believe in all that load of tripe, I'd say *you* jazzed me, rather."

They giggled.

"Okay, it's what I'd wanted to do since the moment I saw you. And I'm glad that I've done it, and that I feel like doing more."

"You can say all these because you are a medical practitioner and you expect to be safe."

Shina smiled. It was this, this sharpness in speaking, not minding if what was spoken was true or not, that forever endeared him to Oye. It would repulse him one day, he knew, but he wanted to see how it would repulse him. He wanted to peel Oye, layer after layer, and reach the vulnerable middle.

"Would you marry me if I asked?" Again, his excitement had sent out the words.

Oye gasped.

"What? Because we fucked and we enjoyed it?"

Shina shook his head. "I know I'm excited and a little disoriented by what just happened, but I'm sane enough to know that I want to live with you every day."

"*Oshay*," Oye sang, snapping his fingers with a queenly flourish. "Like I have no job or something."

Shina finally lip-bit that ear. "You are condescending."

"*Okurrrrr*. You are the five-hundredth person to say that." Oye wriggled with the new frissons from Shina's lips.

"You sound proud of it."

Oye eased out of his arms and walked towards the bathroom. He suddenly stopped by the drawer and pulled out a packet of cigarettes. He made a "do you mind?" face at Shina, who shook his head. He took his time lighting a stick and dragging deeply on it before responding. "Well, what can I say? I have no shame. It's refreshing not to pretend that you don't find it insulting when what is obvious to you is not obvious to everyone else. I mean, commonsense can't be that difficult. It's basic human reasoning. It's annoying when people lack it, and it's double-annoying when they also think a lack of it should inspire a modest response from you. There's not enough time in the whole wide world to be stupid."

Shina rested his head on the headboard. "I know having to deal with people who don't already know obvious things can be mentally exhausting," he said, his tone carefully measured. "But perhaps we should also remember that curiosity is a good thing. It helps us learn and unlearn. Not everyone will already know, or will instantly 'get it'. There was a time we didn't know, and we still do not know. And maybe those who don't have an immediate understanding of the obvious but are asking should not be seen as morally lacking, but simply as people who most probably seek to know."

"Hmm." Oye's hooded gaze was back, this time veiled with a pondering, rather than with a quiet derision. "Okay. I get you. I'll argue better in the future."

Puffs of white smoke snaked into the air.

"Bar Boy." Shina locked his hands above his head and stretched in the bed.

"Excuse you?"

"Nothing."

"If it's 'bad boy' you're trying to say, you'd do well to stop sexifying it, it doesn't sound nice at all. Just say it properly, like 'bad boy' instead of 'baaaaddddd boy', because sometimes we don't realize how much we are being silly when we..."

Shina had left the bed and had come to hold him.

"You don't even respect my gray hairs. Don't you know I'm older than you?"

"Which gray hairs? I don't know your age but you don't look your age."

Oye stubbed out the cigarette and picked up his phone to do a Snapchat reel. Shina peered at him.

"Well, the name fits. You make the house good."

"How?"

"Can I say something?"

"What?" Oye's eyes were still on the phone; he was now pouting and batting his thick eyelashes.

Shina thought of talking, of telling him everything, his marriage, his sons, his divorce. But even as he thought of this, he knew he would not say anything. He would not say anything just yet. "You are so full of stories. Untold stories," he said, crushing Oye's naked belly to his own, feeling a renewed throbbing pressure between his legs. "It's weird how that has a whole different vibe on its own. It makes me feel good."

Oye smiled. "You are a whole mood, you know, Dr Shina."

Shina pulled him closer. "Bar Boy," he moaned. He would not unroll the mat of his past yet.

"Stop calling me that for God's sake! I don't work at the bar!"

"Relax, babe. I call you that because you remind me of my ex. I met him at a bar in Owerri. He used to visit Abuja to see me. He was so slim. He didn't very much like, er, people not, you know, *knowing*. And he had no ass, just like you."

"*Okayyy*, let's ignore the fact that you just body-shamed me, subtly, yeah, but it's still body-shaming. So let me tell you who *you* remind me of."

"Who?"

"All those useless Tops on Grindr. Cliquey, toxic, ego-crazed, entitlement-drunk nitwits with useless fine faces and bodies."

"Uh-oh, babe. That hurt."

"As intended. And you are even calling me 'babe', too! What the actual fuck."

But he couldn't keep on; Shina was already munching on his neck again.

HALF OF A YELLOW AKAMU

(for Joseph Ojadi)

You should hear our feet pitter-pattering down the cleared path to Grandpa's village the moment we leaped out of Papa's car. Our childhood was creamed with gold slants from the sky through the trees, dappling the shade, leaving us giddy and yelling because holidays are brief visits to heaven. My siblings loved climbing the trees in Grandpa's compound, loved the muted tones of his storytelling, loved the way his memories of Grandma overlay each other like carefully folded fond clothes. But I ran for a different reason. I ran for my palmwine tapper. His favorite tree was in the bush behind Grandpa's mud bungalow. He came in the fog, before heat would sear from the sky and close around the palm saplings. A hirsute man glutted in sin, the kind of sin that pockets into abs. His hair spread out on his chest like hands. His back was tighter than the ridges in Grandpa's cassava farm. I could spend millenniums watching him brace up the frightful trees, gourd on shoulder, cutlass in grip. I did not meet him the first time we came to Grandpa's village; Mama said our first visit was when I still lay inside her, curled up, bones forming and heart knowing. The second visit, I was six and aware of my body. It was months before the war. We had just had an early breakfast. Grandpa was still in bed. Mama and Papa, too. I was standing on the verandah letting the breeze play with my eyelashes when Grandpa shuffled out with a chewing stub. He chewed and spat and chewed, and ignored my taunting with a slippery smile. I was about to go in when my palmwine tapper rode up on his bicycle. He came with his materials, greeted Grandpa with a quick bow, and hurried to the tree. I watched his long legs grasp the bole; I imagined the press of his penis against the rough trunk. Things happened in my body. A clutch was in my throat, threatening breath. I wanted to be that tree; I wanted his firm-looking arms encircling me. It occurred to me that the tree might shrug him off. He did not come the following morning, even though I lingered on the verandah till midday, even though I pushed the gates open against Grandpa's instruction and hastened up and down the path to catch him.

I burst into song the day after; my palmwine tapper was cycling up our house. I had left our room before the first rooster in the compound could crow. When my elder brother, Effiom, shuffled up behind me, yawning, I suggested dragging out the giant mattress Grandpa's house-girl put in our room for the holiday, and dropping it at the base of the tree. Effiom conked my head and asked me if eating the mighty boluses of fufu provided at Grandpa's instruction had blocked my brain. Then he hurried out with my cousins from up the river, all of them holding slings and chanting Efik songs from Grandpa's folklore. My palmwine tapper finished his business, rappelled down the tree and gave me a sharp nod before wheeling his bicycle away deeper into the bush. I watched his thighs undulate on the pedals. It emptied sections of my belly, to realize that I could never be his trademark brown shorts, or his low-necked singlet. I would never wrap my skin around him. I would never touch that beautiful body.

My friends from up the river came to call me for soccer. I balked. I knew they needed me—I was easily the best striker. Effiom did not seem interested in football or any kind of sport that did not involve swimming and hunting, so I had fully benefited from Papa's training. Still, I turned away from my friends and asked them to play without me. I wrapped my arms around my body and walked back inside to read a novel, or write yet another play. I ended up falling asleep and dreaming about my palmwine tapper, that he parted his legs for me and I went through those thighs. Afterwards, I lay on his mat—my dream chose a mat—and he entered me back.

I would have continued to have an unruffled moment, an uninterrupted worship of his image graven into my heart. But the war happened. And Ezra came to live in Grandpa's house. And this year, this holiday, this visit, everything changed.

In your dream,

I am a flute in the wind.

Sand clefs in the sun-dead hills

Beckon me to the hollow in your ribs.

But it knifes through my tunes, a

Message carved thereon

For a heart that does not beat

In a boy's body.

•••

My cousin, Ezra, was like those people who use English in a peculiar way, saying, "I wanted going", It's very risk", "Bring the stood", "Don't sigh at adults", "In addy", and I was always correcting him. Perhaps that was why he hated me. Perhaps not. But Ezra's presence made me aware of the very breath that whistled through my nostrils. It bore down on me like Armageddon. He was clumsy and pushy. He invaded my space, talked loudly about girls, asked me if I had a girlfriend already, or if girls had begun to wink at me. I would start to tell him I was only eleven, but he would cut me short with a stentorian cackle. He interrupted everything I hoped to say. He interrupted my yawning. Interrupted my life too many times. He was not tall, was my height, only lankier, my age, too. He was one class ahead of me in his community school and often announced, at every opportunity he got, how he topped his class, with the gloating glee of someone for whom victory was a rarity and not a norm. Yet, he made those silly grammar mistakes. The first time I met him, he had described Papa's car as "bogus".

"Bogus?" I had repeated.

"Yes." And then he went on to curve his arms and wave them to delineate size.

"Oh, you mean 'big'."

He glared at me. "Is something wrong with what I said?"

I sensed trouble brewing. I was surprised to hear him use the word "bogus" like that—when it meant something different entirely—but I shut up. I let it go.

•••

Many centuries ago, before animals lost their speaking voices and there was no special diet and mammals still gave birth to birds, Lion— ruler of the jungle—wanted to select a husband for his daughter, Peahen. She was ravishing, elegant, nice to everyone, and walked around

81

with affable cheer. This made too many prospective suitors come forward to claim her. The betrothal team took them through rigorous stages and was able to pick out the best in three categories: most intelligent, most wealthy and most handsome. The rest could bloody well go to hell.

The ultimate stage was the most dangerous, but it didn't appear so to these shortlisted candidates. They had swum through a pond thick with hungry alligators, carried flames in their bare arms while walking over an abyss, and climbed mountains covered in slime. So this stage was easy. They were ten. Each of them was confident that Peahen was his. Tiger growled his power: *Have you seen my whiskers? Have you seen my fangs? Neat, Baby. You'll run for dear life.* Dog was debonair; he called a feast already. To have come this far was to be ready to get the prize. Flamingo's mind was at rest; who could ever ignore his glamor? And all eyes could see that he and Peahen were as suitable for each other as hair and head. So please. Unicorn looked bored. If it wasn't going to be him, with all his glory, muscles and princely horn, then who? What more could she and her father want?

They were all put to the final test. Only one has to be Peahen's husband; Lion didn't believe in polyandry, even if he himself thrived in polyamory. He asked that a thousand groundnuts be tied in each of ten bags. When no one was looking, he went to the bags and, with his claw, etched each contestant's name at an inconspicuous angle. He called his attendant, whispered to him, and ordered loudly that each eligible suitor be given a bag. Each collected his bag with his name written on it but did not know his name had been written on it. The attendant passed on Lion's requirement: that not more than twenty groundnuts must be eaten from each bag. They were to come back on the third day to drop their bags, which would be assembled for examination.

Positive that there was no way of identifying whose bag was which, these suitors pranced off with their test meal. Many of them gobbled the groundnuts immediately. Dolphin ate two hundred. Elephant stopped at one hundred. Snake swallowed the sixtieth groundnut and rested. Tiger's bag, when he brought it on the third day, hung loose with loss. Dog couldn't even save a single piece from his bag; he had eaten it all.

Only one of these contestants ate exactly twenty groundnuts and let the bag be, despite all temptations.

On the third day, all the animals in the jungle converged in front of Lion's pride rock to watch the finals of the competition. Lion stood up with his darling daughter by his side, roared and said, of all the shortlisted rivals for his daughter's heart, only Tortoise was true to the rule. He ate just twenty groundnuts, and conquered avarice. Overcoming gluttony was overcoming the problem of discontentment. Therefore, he was the best for his daughter.

The animals gaped, the clapping was leaden, but Tortoise crawled forward, sly, intelligent, and claimed his wife.

The real tempest came when Ezra knew about my palmwine tapper. It was a sunny afternoon—the sun is always shining when I think of my palmwine tapper. I was in a light mood. Grandpa had donned me in his *usobo*, which he had rocked on his wedding to Grandma, and I refused to take it off. The night before, placing my sister Daraima on his knobbly but gleaming knee, Grandpa had exulted about how very Catholic Grandma had been, and how he had dropped his ancestors' shrine and become Catholic for her. He said he had no regrets—except, of course, the epiphany he received about his wife not enjoying as much as he did from the faith.

"The problem with this white man's religion," he'd told us, "is that everything we know of it was said by men. Only men. They even gave God their own gender, as if other genders were not in God's image. Any woman who formed as much of an opinion in these books must have been the kind of woman the men agreed with."

He said his epiphany came from the Holy Spirit and so we must not try to fault it. We laughed on the mat spread under the moon. Grandpa's eyes crinkled when he smiled, as if the many nets of his skin were not enough, and his lips formed a merry O, like the mouth of a baby. He must have been cute in his heyday. I wondered if the tale he told us the previous night, the Lion's daughter, was about him and

Grandma. I made a mental note to retell the story in my own way. He caught my eye and kept staring at me as he spoke about the white man's stories of God, as if there was a nuance he intended for me to catch. And then this morning, after rubbing me all over with palm kernel and checking my teeth, he vested me in his wedding clothes and smoothed the twist of the usobo with his little finger, which was bent permanently by a piece of shrapnel that exploded near him during the air raids of two years back. He whispered in my ear that none of his grandchildren had ever worn this particular attire of his. I was prancing on the glimmering edge of this knowledge when Ezra walked in from the river.

"Hey, why are you dressed funny?" he said, his eyes holding a cackle.

He brought sand in and dripped all over the floor, which I had swept that morning. I asked him to get a towel, and he sucked his teeth at me. I was about to say something when my palmwine tapper appeared without his bicycle and tools. I gaped at him. He said he came looking for Etete, my Grandpa.

"Why? He's in his farm with my uncle and aunt," Ezra answered. I bristled at his brusque tone.

"Okay. I just wanted to ask him if he needs some kegs of wine before I exhaust the last one on me," my palmwine tapper said and turned.

I hurried forward. I was worried that Ezra's rudeness had embarrassed him, but not as much as I was that he would leave without talking to me, without knowing my name.

"My name is Akaka. Akakaeno. I am Etete's favorite grandchild. Do you know me? I always wait for you every morning. You look like Van Damme. I like—" I was stuck; Ezra smirked "—I like the way you climb trees and tap wine."

He nodded at me, handsome in his bewilderment, his lips a full rose, his beards a fuzzy growth that chanted spells across to my body, and then—those hairs peeking from under his lilac polo. They made my legs tremble. I wanted him to roll up his shirt. I wanted his nipples in my mouth.

"*Mme ama fi*, I love you," I said under my breath.

He turned swiftly and walked away, waving at Ezra who, from the corner of my eye, had leaned against the wall and folded his arms.

"*Inin,*" I mumbled to the air. Sorry.

My palmwine tapper petered out into a tiny dot. I peered at his back. It suddenly dawned on me that he might have a wife and children at home, that he was bemused by my gushiness. I was certain he would not even remember my name; at best, I was a queer abnormality in his mind: a child growing wrong. Grandpa's wedding dress suddenly became too heavy around my waist. I walked towards my room to divest it.

"You crazy thing."

I stopped.

"You know I've been watching you since you came here."

"I don't understand." I did not turn. I was tethered to the spot.

"There was a time we were sleeping and you caressed up and down my chest, thinking I was too deep in sleep to know."

I turned. He detached from the wall, leaving a dark wet patch on the ochre surface, and ambled toward me.

"*Abasi* saved you that night. I wanted waiting for you to reach my penis before I would lock your hand and deal you a head-butt that would scatter your brains all over the bed. You pervert."

"I don't understand," I repeated. He was lying. I wouldn't touch him with my toenail, let alone place my full palm on his body.

"You will understand when I tell your parents that you are asking an adult to sleep with you at this your age." He shook his head; his disgust was a hideous mask and I was terrified to look at him. "I don't think that poor man heard what you said to him. What do you think he would have done to you if he had heard? Ehh, you fool." His breath fanned my chin, spread upward, as he said the word *fool*. It was musty, male, menacing. I flinched and stepped backward, instinctively.

He scoffed. " 'Etete's favorite grandchild' indeed." His eyes ripped me chest-down, his sneer a blade running through my flesh. I heard my sister's giggle from the backyard where she played in the sand with the village girls. "You better remove this rubbish you put on; you don't even know how you look in it." He roared and went in.

I stared after him, thinking of witchcraft, willing the roof to collapse on his head and flatten him out of my life forever.

•••

He tormented me with this knowledge. He enunciated the story of the inferno that happened in two cities in the bible, Sodom and Gomorra. I was surprised to hear him use that story because the crime committed by the men of Sodom had nothing to do with me or my intentions. But I could say nothing. He kept tabs on me to know where I went, with whom I swam in the river. He threatened me at meal time, watched me carefully to know when Grandpa gave me extra meat and then asked me to pass it to his plate "or else". He told my parents it was a game between us. I had to part with many chunks of meat. Effiom looked dissatisfied. "Don't let that he-goat lure you into silly games," he said to me. "You know he grew up here; don't let him cheat you." I was mum, afraid I would burst into tears if I opened my mouth.

"None of them have eyes in those their big heads," Ezra said to me one evening after we had taken turns to bathe before bed. "Even that your brother, with all his city bossiness and ITK, cannot see what is sitting right upon his nose. Imagine! I can still excuse outside your sister; she's only five, and cannot be able to be aware of such things yet. Her brother is full of mischief that is bigger than his years."

I sat bolt upright. "Ezra."

"What is it?"

"Whose big heads? Are you talking about my parents like that?"

He sucked his teeth. "Who mentioned your parents? Only Abasi knows the kind of demonic movies you watch in your big city house on your big city television. I will soon find out all what is really causing all this. But first, I will deal with you. It is not in my presence you will do this to your parents. It is not in my presence you will do this."

And he turned his back.

"Don't touch me *o*. In fact, I will ask James the blacksmith to make me a pair of metal panties so that I can be able to wear when you sleep in the same room with me."

I choked on my unshed tears. His words, accentuated by his bad grammar, thundered in my ears. I could not close my eyes until I heard the first rooster crow.

•••

Ezra did not stop. Things intensified, and I finally broke. We were at the village well one morning when he began to taunt me for hanging my hand like a girl's while handling the scooper. He said people who wanted to change the gender God gave them would not make heaven, because they were spitting on God's creation. Everyone there hollered with laughter. I dropped the scooper, a thick black leather affair, and tried to pace my breathing as I spoke.

"I know your sins, too, Ezra. You have been stealing Etete's money. Yes! You've been stealing from him to give those boys from up the river to help you get used military boots from their store. I wonder what you want to use the boots for."

All eyes turned to him in one movement.

"That's not all o," I pressed on. "You also masturbate to Aunty Faith's picture in Grandpa's room. You think I don't see you?"

Ezra lunged forward, his metal bucket clanging, and covered my mouth. His parents died in the Nigeria-Biafra war. His maternal aunt took him in and enrolled him in the new government school established in Mbo, where she taught mathematics. Grandpa said such a woman was rare, that she reminded him of his late daughter-in-law, and that she should bring him a piece of her as his sight was failing. He needed to keep her close, next to the memory of his son's wife. So she brought a picture of her, taken with an imported camera before the war, and hung it in Grandpa's room. I found it funny a keepsake, since Grandpa could barely see.

Ezra knew about all this. I did not know he felt that way about his aunt until I caught him through the chink in the window, several times, holding the picture in one hand and jerking the other between his thighs furiously until a growl rose from him. Effiom had once told me about how something came out of him during his sleep, something viscid and milky, and how what he saw in his sleep involved a girl he crushed on in his class. Effiom said the incident intrigued him, because he didn't even have to masturbate as usual. *Masturbate.* I had never heard the word before. Efiom explained to me, but I was too scared to do it. What if blood came out instead? I waited once upon a time to see that same fluid burst from between Ezra's legs. I waited and waited until I realized that he was my age and boys of my age did not release stuff like that yet.

"So this boy can talk loudly like this," someone in the water line said.

A lump sat in the base of my throat. I was not that kind of person, and I despised Ezra for making me splash outward like that. I felt even smaller. "*Daga!*" I yelled, slapping his hand off my mouth. "*Sana mi yak*, leave me alone!"

I grabbed my bucket unfilled and stalked off. People clapped, hailing me. But I knew who had won between Ezra and me. It was Ezra who, when Grandpa died years later and we were throwing sand on his coffin behind his house, would whisper to me, his eyes concealed behind dark glasses—"Who knows maybe your abomination killed him before his time; maybe he caught wind of it and his poor heart couldn't handle it"—and my crying would pause. It was Ezra who would later attend the same secondary school with me, who would tell his friends about me, who would lead them to clap behind me and sing songs of mockery and say, "If we catch you touching anyone in this hostel, we will break your bones." It was Ezra who would always come to my class or my dormitory and peer over my shoulder to see what I was scribbling. "Don't let me catch you writing nonsense o, or else!" He capped off his threats with that phrase: "or else". It always cracked a line through my chest and made my pen hand tremble for long after he had gone.

It was Ezra who would come to my bunk one day before prep and prise the paper I was writing on from my hand. I would sigh, relieved that it was not my Chemistry textbook. "*Ami mme uma fien,* my palmwine tapper"—I would have written in the inner flap of my Chemistry textbook.

"What the fuck is this?"

"It's a poem for a girl, Ezra."

"Really?" He would raise the paper. "Is this a poem? Tell me. You must be silly to think an Arts student will not know to tell the genres apart. You, a science student, too. You have guts *sha*!"

I would drop my head in my hands, the creative words in my head vanishing forever, unable to ingrain themselves in less nebulous forms on paper anymore.

"This is a story, prose."

"I know, Ezra."

"So why did you lie?" He would read a few more lines. "You're writing about men in love with men?"

I would be silent.

"Finally. A proof. I'm so going to tell your parents on the next visit so they would know the kind of son they have."

He would start walking off with the paper. I would scramble after him. People would watch from their bunks, their expressions puzzled.

"*Mbok*, Ezra. Please. I promise not to write it again. In fact, bring it, let me tear it up right now. I swear never to write such a thing again."

"Rest. Men in love with fellow men? In this part of our world? Such a story doesn't exist, Akakaeno; you can't catch it." He would fling the paper in my direction. It would dance before I swiped it in my palms. I would pray, again, that he stop.

He would not stop.

My bunkmate, Odion, who would have known about me, would storm in one afternoon, after Ezra was done, and call me names and say I was too soft, that if he had been the one, he wouldn't let anyone talk him down like that. "You gays are always apologizing," he would later whisper, "that's why we straights can walk over you anyhow." I would want to correct him that it was "gay people" and not "gays", and that the idea of "straight" was simply a laughable thing to picture. I would say none of this. I would sit instead on my bed, my eyes on my big Milo

92

tin, thinking—and failing—to understand how possible it was for anyone on earth to catch a story that did not exist.

But that late afternoon—after the episode at the well—the sun slanting its roseate glow into the verandah, I wasn't thinking about any story. I was blank. Ezra placed a bowl filled with a yellow pudding before me. He called it *akamu*, said it was what the Igbo called it. He said it was one of the reasons he must marry an Igbo girl.

"Is this a bribe?"

"Come on." He smiled. His smile looked like a grimace.

I did not smile. "You want to kill me?"

"I'm just trying to protect you here. If I wanted killing you, I would have done that."

"I see."

He picked up a machete and dragged it over the mud pillar. Scrapes of earth bounced. "I just want the best for you."

"You don't *know* the best for me." I stamped my foot. This anger was new, fresh, foreign. For the first time, I was not mad at him; I was mad at something else.

"He is not for you," he said.

The anger whooshed out of me. I sighed, suddenly deflated. "I know."

"Go on, I didn't poison it."

"*Sosono sonono eti eti,*" I said as I took the first spoon. It melted on my tongue with a sour bite. Later, it tasted sweet. "Thank you."

•••

The evening my palmwine tapper caught Grandpa at home, he told Grandpa that he was going to Port Harcourt, that his friend had found him a job as a security man in one of the oil refineries. He would be moving with his family. Grandpa laid his shivering hands on his head and prayed. Every "Amen" from my palmwine tapper's lips tugged a chunk from my heart. Grandpa prayed for a long time. He ended his blessings with "*Tie sun*, goodbye."

My palmwine tapper hugged him, dropped five full kegs of wine by the bench, and turned. In the failing light, he looked angelic, gilded in the sunset's glow, a god disappearing into nightfall.

"*Sana sun*, safe journey," I called after him, but he didn't reply. Nor did he look back. *He is not for you.*

Grandpa was stroking the red cap of one of the kegs. He used his curled finger. I wanted to take it and straighten it, smooth it, return it to what it was. But I knew I could only break it. I took the kegs in.

I did not see my palmwine tapper again till we left Grandpa's village that holiday.

•••

Holidays ended. Ezra, Effiom and I washed the car while Papa and Mama said their goodbye and "Take your drugs and meal at the right time, Etete. And stop going to the farm; we won't stop sending you weekly allowance" to Grandpa. Effiom had just splashed his last on the bonnet and dropped his bucket when Ezra started scoffing.

"What is your problem?" Effiom barked.

"Not yours apparently," Ezra returned. "So don't bother."

"Don't speak to my brother like that." I sounded too limp, too contrived.

Irritated, Effiom flounced away. I heard him telling Daraima to stop doing something and start doing something, because time was going. I imagined telling him about Ezra and me. But I knew it was too late. The first permission of slavery is the worst.

"You and your parents are returning to Uyo this afternoon." Ezra turned to me, his jute sponge dripping. "I wager they don't see what I can see in their son."

"The same way Grandpa can't know what I know about his grandchild," I returned through gritted teeth, my voice low so nobody would hear. "Just imagine what it would do to him to learn that his eleven-year-old grandchild wants to sleep with the woman who gave him a new life. Mr Wager."

"Hey, hey, don't go saying nonsense there o." He waved his sponge at me, hastening away, his hand and voice quavering. Water drops landed on my face.

•••

The car doors were open, on Papa's instruction. He played an evergreen Efik song. Grandpa was clutching Effiom and Daraima to his chest in the doorway. I looked around to take in Udung Uko, the huts, the river, the bluish mountains, the trees, the tree my palmwine tapper had loved like a woman. It was as though people were walking in time to the song, a kind of quiet, concordant dance. Till today, when I catch the strains anywhere of that song Papa was playing on his car stereo the day we left, I feel a pang in my chest.

I sat next to Papa. Mama sat in the back with Effiom and Daraima. I did not turn to wave at Grandpa; I didn't want to catch Ezra's face by mistake. When the car slipped into the path flanked by heavy-foliage trees, I stared out the window.

Mama yawned from the back. "I'm too tired; you'll cook dinner when we get home."

I heard Daraima clap her hands *kpra-kpra-kpra*. "Thank God," Effiom said with a whoop. I looked at the trees whipping past and smiled. The load in my chest was loosening.

Papa nodded. "I wanted to complain. But these kids find my meals irresistible enough."

"Complain? Don't be a lazy husband."

They laughed. They jibed like this all the time. Mama had stolen my line; I was supposed to say what she said. Papa noticed.

"My boy, what happened? You are unusually quiet."

"I'm fine, Papa."

"Akaka is fine," Mama said. "He is just missing his Etete already."

I trailed my pinky down the curve of the glass. *They don't see what I can see in their son.*

Soon, we reached a checkpoint. The federal soldiers poked their guns into the car and peered about as if they would catch any rebel insignia. Then they told Papa to give them some "kola". When they waved us through, Papa laughed.

"These feds are just hungry for power," he said. "The war ended and we are here and they don't feel good about missing all the thrills they had while bombing the Igbo to dust."

Mama slapped a mosquito off. "At least, they would be the first to assume we are part of the Igbo."

"It is not an assumption. We were all in the war."

"I know."

I was supposed to talk, I knew. This was the moment I chipped in a line, similar to a line I would later glean, decades later, from the colorful TELL magazines in Papa's study, about "the neofascist regime and its failing desperation to reassert power and autonomy", a line I would use and use, because it sounded intelligent and way beyond my years and broadened Papa's smile. "He's so current in the affairs of our country," he would boast to his friends, his voice lilting with pride. "He has the heart of a leader."

"What a precocious boy you have," his friends would reply. "And he's also socially conscious! You are doing a good job on them."

They always flocked at our house, denouncing the coups and the lingering smoke of the war, refusing to call it "civil war" like the BBC did. They rehashed pretty much what was in the decadent newspaper columns, only in harsher tone. They condemned the market raids, the railway traders raids, the confiscation of people's sweat, the decrees that turned landlords into empty-bellied vagrants and rats into landlords. Suffering was lucid in my land, clear in its helplessness. The hair of children turned copper, their bellies looked like distended leaves. All activism rose and died in the nooks of friends' houses, not even beer parlors anymore, because more soldiers left their barracks and drank at bloody civilian pubs. And if you as much as stared a soldier in the face, he whipped you like a cow. My classmate said his father was ordered out of his car to lie flat on the road, and thrashed on his buttocks because he dared break the curfew. He said his father had been rushing his grandmother to the hospital. They asked the aged woman to come down and do frog jumps so her son would be released. My father's friends had similar tales to share, and as they railed in Papa's parlor, I wrote more poems. Poems I was certain I would never publish. Poems I knew I would never show anyone. I would later contact a publishing company from my home in Connecticut and release them when, in decades, another uniformed menace would arise in my country and call themselves SARS, this time targeted at successful, flamboyantly dressed young people and their families.

But right then, in the car, I only remembered the bowl of akamu Ezra had placed before me, the shadow on the verandah darkening one half and leaving the other brightly yellow. It was the same way the sun had covered one part of my palmwine tapper's leg. I turned to Papa behind the wheel. "If I become the head of this country, I will make my people smile."

He smiled. Mama smiled, too. I was sure they didn't understand me in full. Daraima gawked at me with her large eyes. Efiom turned up his nose as if someone had spoiled the air. I wondered if Ezra had said anything to him. I had no reason to wonder; I just did. My heart was racing and it was not from fear.

The sky deepened. Mama asked Papa to lower the volume of the song. She started to pray against armed robbers. They were now like mosquitoes on these roads, and they had a soft spot for a big car and a happy family. We closed our eyes, except Papa behind the wheel. We said *Amen* solemnly. Mama prayed until the five-minute track ran four times over. Papa said the people she should have prayed against were the soldiers tearing our country apart: they were the real armed robbers. I watched a short pregnant woman hurry across the road and wondered if there were armed robbers on the road to Port Harcourt and exactly how much would take me there.

•••

The next day was Sunday, the first day of the week, of the month, too. It was Thanksgiving service, for Etete's well-being, for a safe journey, for a lurid school resumption. I stood in the church with the opaque colored glass and, as the choir sang slow-meter hymns, I wept for my palmwine tapper. Mama held my head to her hip and wiped my face. The women bedecked in gold turned to me and smiled, their headgears flaring. They all thought I was weeping because of Jesus' grace.

TELL MAMA YOU LIKE BOYS

I am 25 years old, just blossoming into responsibility. And my mama has just named my first bit: Get married.

I didn't understand, the day she first pressed it. I really didn't understand. I wanted to. But I didn't ask for an explanation. I *don't* ask for explanations. I simply zip up my words in my dirty old bag of silences. Then I let the days slip through my fingers.

This time, she has raised the issue again, on the uncompleted top floor of my father's house, the night a grim, grave enfolding around me, sheathing my secrets. Her eyes are firm; she's tired of my hide and seek. And I know I will have to unzip that dirty old bag.

And let everything spill to the floor.

Every damn thing.

"Mama, I'm not thinking of marriage. I'm…" But I stop.

I spill nothing. How do I say it? How do I say such a thing?

I simply drag down the zip, let a few silences become words, soft slippery embodiments, and rise into the dark air, their ghost nebulous bodies saying nothing; then I run the zip closed again.

My mama is watching.

Waiting.

She needs to know.

So I complete it.

Safely.

"...I'm a career man."

Silence.

"And so?" she asks. "Career men don't have marriage prospects?"

"They don't all the time, mama." My tone is becoming stiff, stringy, stretched by years of whispered longings. Even to my own ears. "To them, their job comes first. They are more committed to their work than to any romantic relationship."

She hums. "I see. And they don't marry?"

"Mama, marriage is not always the next step. It is a choice."

Her eyes widen into luminous discs in the night air. I sigh. I thought I had prepared myself for this drama. "So you are saying you won't marry?"

"Mama,"—if my sanity were a balcony rail, I would hold it, I would grip it—"marriage is a wonderful state of partnership, but I will marry when I want."

"And when is that?"

"Mama, I'm just 25 years old! I don't even have a steady job yet!"

Silence floats out again, but this time from my mama's bag, a wordless, bloodless silence. She is peering at me, looking for a way of clothing it in words. She has done it many times here. This is where she comes up at night to put shapeless thoughts in ill-fitting words and send them to God. Her prayer space. Her war room.

I am tired of her failures.

"What is it, Mama?"

"You don't even have a girlfriend," she says, calmly.

"What?"

"You don't even have a girlfriend," she repeats, still weaving her words with that arcane calm. I feel like melting into the unfinished, algae-covered wall behind me. "I have never seen you with a girl. I don't know whether you have ever fallen in love before. Even your younger brother, who is just 19 years old, brings his girlfriends home."

I look into the dark, blindly, flailing to catch a grasp. A saving. Fornication is more acceptable when it is not a recorded abomination. I knew it would come to this. I expected it, but I did not want to. The presence of a girlfriend is enough to allay a mother's growing fears that one might be homosexual. It is useless to wonder if she would ever think I could really be bisexual. Or a liar.

Mothers want girlfriends. Girlfriends must also become wives.

I can't handle either.

"Mama, I don't understand you," I lie after drawing another blank. "I thought I told you about Titi—"

"You didn't show me this Titi. You just told me there was a girl called Titi. I didn't hear you call her on the phone; I didn't hear her call you. She lives in Lagos, and you live here. And I have not seen you travel to Lagos at all. The only thing you told me afterwards was that you had broken up with her."

I look far away from her discs, because they are like loaded guns muzzled against my chest. About to jerk pure evil. I want to search the night for egress. But everywhere is so dark. And my bag so heavy.

Heavy with silences.

I break one again.

"Mama, Titi may be past tense. But at least I dated her."

"You broke up with a girl no one had ever seen you date. You dated a girl I didn't know, even after it was over." She is bulleting me now.

"Must you know about her? What difference would it have made now since we are no more together?"

"It would have made me stop wondering—" She stops herself, too. Her bag shrinks back into hiding, a lopsided accusation.

I do not pursue the matter. I make as if to go.

"Oh, you will walk out on me?"

"No, mama"—a sullen denial.

"Just because I'm telling you about your life!"

"Mama, I know. I'm also thinking about my life."

"You don't!" she fires. "And you aren't! Look at you! Look at Desmond! Look at Moyo! Look at Tunji! Uche! All the boys you went to school with. Even Dimeji that had women problems is getting married next week!"

"Mama, I'm not Dimeji—"

"Shut up and let me finish! Your mates are already doing big-big things, settling down and moving on with their lives!"

I hate it, hate it so much, when she forgets who I am, when she measures my life with the tape rule of others' lives. But then I realize, with a sharp stab of melancholy, that she doesn't even know me. She doesn't know me at all.

"Mama, marriage is not 'a big-big thing'. At least not in the sense of what you mean. It is not an achievement."

I am trying so hard to keep my bag, to not raise my voice at her and dump it on her head.

"I see! When will you have your own children? Or you don't want to have children?"

"Of course, I want to have my kids." The bag shifts in my grasp, wriggling for escape. I crush it down. "I'm going to have my own kids." I want to say more, about how having children is something we are given and not something we take, but I hold the zipper up. Silence is still a shield, no matter what they say. Especially when the night is so dark and full of eerie things.

"Then what is stopping you?"

"Mama, nothing is stopping me. I just have things to set in place first. At the right time, all these things will fall into place."

"Shut up! You think I'm growing younger?" she rains on me, and I imagine my torso opening up, my chest spurting, becoming red.

Oh. This is about *her*. This is about her having grandkids. I slowly start to unzip the bag, and stop.

"Mama, if it's grandchildren you want, Lekan is there to give you some."

"Listen to yourself! You even want your younger brother to marry before you do? *Oluwa!*"

I pull down the zipper a little more, and words bounce out.

"He doesn't have to marry. People don't need to marry someone first before they can have a child."

"*Olorun mi koo!* My God forbid!" She is snapping the abomination over her head, behind her, into a void known only to her. I want to chuckle. I am now enjoying the darkness of it all. "My Creator rejects it that my sons have children with harlots and homeless women!" Her own bag bursts open. "And if it is gay you want to do, tell us, let us *kuku* know!"

"Mama!"

My amusement wipes off, leaving a temptation. An open space. A time and a place for me to unlock my bag fully and upturn all the silences into the dark. Where they will become words.

Words close things off.

Words also create new beginnings.

Words will free me. They will seek to bind me, yes, but it will only feel like that because they have set me free.

The night will go.

And if it doesn't, I will at least be able to see what is in it.

And I can also tell her people don't 'do gay', that there are asexual gay people, that people are simply gay, whether they have sex or not, whether they marry a man or not.

But I hold my bag fast.

I say nothing.

I let the night deepen its hue.

I let the silence enclose me and her.

In a single spool of knowledge.

She knows.

I know she knows.

But she dares me to tell. She dares me to live in her face.

And even though now, a silence speaks in my bag, whispering an instruction, I know I will never gift it the liberating clothing of words. I will never adorn it. I am a dependent 25-year-old Nigerian, living in my parents' house, and I'm gay.

HUNTING FOR FIREFLIES: A GRASP AT A FADING SANITY

Your husband microwaved your baby.

You were a lawyer in your lifetime. Before the SSMPA bill made it to the second reading at the National Assembly at all, your husband would rake his talon-like fingernails down your cheeks and down to your throat and pummel you until your eye swelled into an aubergine. He blew up your baby boy the Thursday after that day, the 7th of January, 2014, people still saying "Happy new year" to each other in one moment, and in the next, President Goodluck Ebele Jonathan climbing the rostrum to tell every non-heterosexual human in Nigeria that it was time to shrink into a living carcass. He stuffed the slender one-and-a-half-year-old—the boy already learning to call you "Mama", already smart enough to help you adjust your court wig and fetch your car keys—your husband stuffed him in the microwave after another round of thumping you in the master bedroom. You heard the implosion from upstairs. You rushed down in your nightdress. The machine's door lolled open, mangled. Blood had splattered everywhere—on the serving spoon, on the silverware, on the casseroles; mixed into your chicken stew, the tiled wall, the Formica table. You poured the chicken stew over the fence and flung the pot after it. You knew, as you soaked the other utensils in Omo later, that you could never scrub your son's blood and intestines and brains out of their bodies. So you dropped everything in the backyard and set it ablaze.

•••

You met your husband at a commissioner's party. The city was thick with vagabonds, and the Honorable was having yet another housewarming, as though to tell the people to complain a little more loudly. You were gossiping and laughing about this with your friends —all of them lawyers, too, immersed in the falsehoods of what was right and what was not—when a man keeled over and splashed the contents of his red cup on you. The reddish liquid soaked into your green wrap dress. There were gasps all around— *the lawyer who got wet, isn't that ju-eesy*—and you were rearing to drop all your sodden dignity and deal him a hot slap when another man took your elbow, gently, coaxingly, and led you away. He found a towel and dried you up. He was the drunk man's friend, he said. His name was Ofonime. He offered to buy you a meal, if you didn't mind. He hoisted his palms and swore it was for nothing else, just an apology date. But you didn't believe him. You said to yourself, "Can a man really be this nice without ulterior motives?" You took his niceness for interest. You should have believed him.

A date led to more, most of which were initiated by you. He seemed to grow distant, to become more handsome day by day, more laid-back, more irresistible. Sometimes, he gave one limp excuse or the other. Other times, he came. You were surprised when he didn't call you to ask if you'd reached home. You figured it out for yourself: he must have been too tired after the whole day to use his phone. It didn't matter that his status on BB chat was always reading active. He needed his rest, since his diurnal hours were always busy. He was still job-hunting, a second-class upper graduate of Chemical Engineering from UNICAL. He wore a shirt and a tie every morning and roamed Calabar till sundown, his credentials clutched to his hip in a My Clear Bag, his throat dry, his belly hollow with disillusionment. His shoes gathered the dust of the city. It was lobbying for a job that had brought him to the commissioner's party, he told you. You said you would put in a word with your boss at the Chambers where you worked; his friend owned a juice manufacturing industry and perhaps he could work there. He latched his arms around you and said he had always seen it in your eyes how much you felt for him; that he had only been quiet because he didn't want to jump the gun and break the friendship you two had. But the truth was, he lied. You didn't know. You were too delirious with accomplishment to read his eyes and see the invented glow in them, invented just for you so you could get working to fix him up quickly.

On his birthday, you sat up all night so you could be the first to text him and call him and sing and upload his pictures on Facebook and Instagram. You had a divorce case the next morning and you needed all your faculties in attendance, but you didn't think not sleeping well for one night would have any inimical effect on your court coordination. You halved your paltry wages and sent him steady credit alerts—even when he said you shouldn't bother, that he had "an uncle" who kept him fine. He was telling you everything about himself but you were too starry-eyed to look down and see what was going on.

You were hunting for fireflies, and they were beautiful when you caught them in a glass bowl—in your mind.

The first time you kissed him, he pulled his lips away, sharply, instinctively, and you saw in his eyes the wounded patina of the violated. It was like raping a client. You asked him if he was a virgin. You expected him to laugh, because the idea of a man being a virgin was against The Alpha Male Code. But he did not laugh. He only shrugged and asked you if you would like to play Ludo.

One night, you invited him to your two-room flat in Ekpo Abasi. He came with a friend who later disappeared after you went in and came out in your sexy lingerie. It worked, the lingerie. He said you had chased his friend away. You said, Good for the friend. What did he bring company for? You didn't know how a man couldn't take the cue from a woman who asked him over to her place at night. You took him in your hand. But he remained limp and mumbled something about how it wasn't right. It wasn't right to sleep with you just because you bought him designer shirts and shoes and were also helping him to secure a job. It wasn't right to take advantage of you like that. He suggested a sex toy, said he knew exactly where to get it for you if you were too embarrassed to get it yourself. You drew back and asked him if he was impotent. His eyes flickered with a flame that made you step back completely. He foamed at the mouth while telling you that he could get hard right there and then if he wanted to, that impotence did not even have anything to do with a soft dick, that impotence was about semen not having strong sperms in it. That he had strong sperms. You ignored the absence of truism in his words. You catwalked back toward him and dared him to show you his strong sperms. Bring your boss here, let me fuck him—he said. The air paused. Your A/C stopped breathing. The muted images on the Plasma television hanging on the wall froze. You started cackling and he joined you hesitantly and you picked up your wine glass and thumped his shoulder and said he should consider joining a comedy crew.

The next night you lured him into your abode, you were prepared for him. You dropped methamphetamine into his drink and dragged him to bed. You were on top, gliding, feeling his dick engorge and lengthen inside of you, when he suddenly came awake and, with silence trickling out of his eyes, regarded you with all the hate inside him. His mouth was open in the saddest shock you'd ever seen. You wanted to climb down immediately, but you were on the verge of exploding, so you stayed there until you could arch your back and stab the night with a sharp cry.

He ignored your calls for weeks.

He only picked up after you sent him a text that his application at the juice manufacturing industry had been reviewed and that he was to come for an exclusive interview on the following Monday. He went, got the job, came back, kissed you passionately, knelt before you, and proposed to you.

You held him to your chest and cried. In the cathedral, in your silk white wedding dress, you cried, too.

You tried for a child for years. His touch, fumbly at the beginning of the marriage, became even klutzier as time went on. He wouldn't kiss you, or look at your face, or fold your legs into 99 positions; he would just lie on top of you and shut his eyes and grunt *ha-ha-ha*, cumming in seconds. It was like making love with a spirit; there was no soul, no link. He stopped asking you if you had come. He simply climbed down, rolled away and got up to go into the bathroom, where he would lock himself for long minutes, until you faded into a tired sleep. Sometimes, he came home at midnight. Sometimes, he didn't come home at all, didn't eat at home either, and when he did come home, he oozed a strange perfume.

Parents from both families were already grumbling, particularly his mother. He was her only child and she needed this grandchild more than anyone else. Her visits and probing were incessant. She was always coming with a bottle of herbal decoctions or a black soap wrapped in papyrus, and inviting you to see strangely dressed dreadlocked men living in the creeks. You went with her; you drank the bilious brews; you swam in the banana grove river, naked—with all your lawyer knowledge.

Finally, the fifth year with your husband, you peed over a stick and watched it tell you you were pregnant.

You wept.

•••

You pushed the boy out in a lemon-scented hospital and named him Nsikak. Nothing was impossible. Your fireflies bowl was getting full. You did not think the worst could be possible as well. He loved that child the way he loved his feces. He would rather not see his feces, but at least if he saw a shaman packing it into his diabolical bag, he would fight for it.

•••

Why?—you asked him now, without tears, leaning on the door jamb, your hands still wet, your nightdress still smelling of smoke from the backyard. *Why?* Like asking about colors that one shouldn't wear. *Why?* Like being curious about someone's decision not to bleach their skin. *Why?* The reason he gave was similar to the one he gave for always hitting you. *This marriage sucks. I feel like you robbed me of my real life. Everything that makes this sham appear real and permanent must be destroyed.*

You were used to lying; when your family and colleagues asked you about your aubergine eye and bruised cheeks, you told them you sleepwalked often and had to bump into hard things before your husband awoke and rescued you. It had always been easy for you to say outrageous things, to concoct absurdities, and repeat them until they became truths. You told everyone who asked that it was a fire accident: the boy had traipsed into the kitchen one unguarded afternoon, stood on a stool, switched on the gas stoves and struck a match. It did not matter how plausible the story was, how a boy barely two years old could do all that. But it was simply enough that everybody thought Nsikak smart enough to do anything. The funeral was dismal; the family gathered at Saint Barnabas Anglican Church and you buried his intestines and bits of brain and skull in a small coffin.

Your bowl cracked and the flies drifted out.

Your husband stopped coming home on weekends. You could no longer weep. He had gone off the railings, in a way that stranded logic and defied challenge. It was like living under a military dictator, steeped in inhuman decrees, terror rather than reason ruling. You were tired. He wrested a signature from you, went to the bank and asked that your joint account be split. He had asked you to prepare for a divorce—Sheybi you're a lawyer, he said. Do what lawyers do. Break this vow in court. It was never supposed to happen. Your father said he never saw any good in him. Your mother, a retired lecturer in a wheelchair, sobbed on your shoulders and asked you, Uduak, what have you done with your life? What did you marry? You wondered how many of your lies they actually believed. His mother would clutch you and shake you and ask, How did you offend him? *How* did you offend your husband?

You didn't know what to say. You simply didn't know the man you married. Or maybe you knew him, but you would rather convince yourself that you didn't, that the only thing that qualified a marriage to hold was a mature man and a mature woman. You were simply fulfilling natural law. He may not have wanted you, but he was *supposed* to want you. Right? Men should want women, as is written in all books.

•••

That January, when the SSMPA law was finally passed into constitution, you were surprised, because you knew many inner-circle legislators that the law would chain and dispossess, legislators who frequented gloomy, smoke-filled clubs where faceless men did strip-tease and slid down poles, where woke university boys sucked dicks. He came home that Monday evening (after a long spell of absence) —he must have watched the news somewhere—he came home with red in his eyes. He entered your study, where you lay trying to recover the energy lost on brooding rather than on sleeping, and yanked you up by the tails of your braids. He dragged you like that to the balcony overlooking the parlor and, for a terrible moment, you believed he wanted to hurl you down. But he rushed downstairs, grabbed the remote, switched on the TV and asked you to watch. Every news channel was broadcasting the imperative new law. You could barely read the headlines through your tears and snot: *Same-Sex Marriage (and Related Acts) Prohibition Act Signed Today. We Come Against Sodom and Gomorrah Acts in our Beloved Country. No Western Immorality to be Condoned.* He

114

banged on the radio on the window ledge: every station was screaming about the same thing. It suddenly became the most important thing in the nation, who and who wanted to get married or sleep together. The barbarities of Boko Haram suddenly no longer mattered. Insurgency and economic meltdown became secondary. You wondered why the "adult-marry-child" legalities in the nation did not gather as much mêlée.

He yelled at you that what kind of stupid laws were you and your kind interpreting. *Sixteen!*—he hollered—*Sixteen international human rights groups signed a letter condemning this bill, yet these guys went ahead! Hear what Mass Resistance is saying! "Taking bold steps to fight back all ploys to subvert public morality"—just imagine. What do they know about public morality? What is morality? Taking people's lives? Hear people rejoicing. How can you not see this as a fundamental human right issue?* He mentioned his secondary-school mates and university co-alumni, people whose penises he had once popped with his mouth and who were now called to the bar. He asked you what they would now do, if they would do anything, questions to which you didn't have enough answers. He stabbed the throw pillows with every broadcast. You wondered why he was so worked up. Had he expected a pat on the back? Before the law, he never had peace with himself. Before the law, men caught together had always been dragged into open streets, stripped, beaten and burned. Same for the women doing unspeakable things with each other. This was Nigeria, didn't he know? Or maybe the catchphrase "This is Nigeria" only became valid *after* the law. Maybe the law exacerbated things.

The following evening, he squeezed your son into the microwave.

115

Your fireflies were now all over the place. They had fangs like snakes and bit you all over. Everything became traps. You didn't know whether you should move forward, how, where. You heard the catchphrase making the rounds of Nigeria, like wildfire—"14 years!"—and your heart jumped up your throat. At the Chambers, you rocked backward on your high heels and leaned against your table for support as your colleague, Tolani, sang it. She drummed on her desk, her girlish giggles counterpointing with the beats. Her dollish eyes snapped with an excitement you couldn't understand. 14 years? How come? The proposed bill had called for five years—so where did 14 years come in? You found the rumors incoherent. You found the law itself incoherent. A crime harms people and endangers proprietorship. *What did people's consensual sexual affairs have to do with that?* you asked your mirror reflection. At first, no one was convicted—even the Nigerian advocate who had always been involved in pro-LGBTI+ demonstrations and repeatedly arrested by the police was ignored. But, later, 42 young people were raided at a party in Lagos and charged to court. You saw the barristers swarm into your chambers that day to discuss the hot case with your boss, who was a SAN. You rushed home that evening and ran a cold bath. You prayed that your husband never come home. Or that he come with his friends. When he came with his friends, there was no battering—they only sat in the parlor, eating the fried snails and Hennessy you served them, yelling about Champions Leagues, or about the kinds of men they slept with: which one did not know how to eat Shawarma; which one had the nerve to cook *afia efere* with their wife in the kitchen, saying "My cousin's wife, don't put oil at all o, plus the crayfish is enough *mbok*, my cousin doesn't like seafood that much"; the Catholic priest who wanted a threesome and was actually your husband's boyfriend, and then your

116

secret favorite, the doe-eyed boy who stole their imported jewelry during a hotel tryst and absconded overnight. They used idiolects—*sagba*, *TB*, *Lola*, *Kito*, words you couldn't begin to picture. At work, you turned away from your colleagues when they talked about the Arrested 42, recoiling into the secret crimes of your home. They were later released on bail, but your world had rent in the middle. No center holding. Your colleagues, out of exasperation, stopped asking you what was going on. There were holes inside you that would never be filled. Your last checkups on earth, the doctors told you that your chances of giving birth again were slim, because your fertility was low.

Your bowl was empty. Your fireflies could not be grasped, could never be grasped again, even if you left the marriage and gave witness to all his crimes.

"Take a people's human right and watch them turn to beasts," you said to the magistrate in your last court session. Then you bowed out.

You had defended a woman who killed her husband, a wife beater. She had poisoned him. She used Gammalin 20. You bought the Gammalin 20, two bottles, during one of those weekends you knew he would be sleeping out, so that when he came back, he would not find you anymore. You gulped them undiluted, two of them, fast, gurgling. Your life had been a melodrama from the start, and you were such a remarkable actress. You crumpled onto your bedroom floor, the room in which you had first climbed him. As your eyes closed, you still saw Nsikak in your half-dreams, your beautiful son, his cleft chin jutting out as he smiled and said, "Mama, wig is fine."

GENERATION TO GENERATION

MEMUNAT

My daughter's school looms up, washed with the morning's glow, and I remember my husband saying the facility maintenance fee imputed in the bill is "too much". I have told him it is not. Nothing is too much for our daughter. He knew everything before he insisted we have her. How many times does he visit the school, anyway? I pause at the open gates to let a bunch of girls and boys scamper past, a severe-looking woman in a sharp striped suit bringing up the rear. She's new, because I had never seen her. Or maybe she's not new, since the last Open Day was ages past. Her smile and "Asbi, is that your mum?" startle me. My daughter, dimpling like hip pockets, says "Yes, ma'am." Her Capri-Sonne straw is pointed awkwardly at her nose. She has been careful enough not to let anything spill on her hijab. I watch the woman. She nods at me and I nod back. She walks off with the pupils.

"Asbirullah."

"Yes, mummy?"

"Is that your English language teacher? The one you said sometimes replaces your pocket money when it gets stolen in class?"

My daughter giggles. "Yes, mummy." She drags out the *Yes* and pulls through her straw.

"Remind me to see her before I leave."

"Okay, mummy." She grips the straw with her lips and draws until a dry, scraping noise fills the car.

"I have told you to stop doing that." I reply to the gatekeeper's nod and nose towards the hibiscus rows. "Classy human beings don't slurp on their drink so noisily."

"Ouch," she says, her lower lip pushed out. "Sorry, mummy."

I chuckle. She knows. She only did that to irritate me. It's the same way she snatches my meat during supper and I have to chase her up the stairs to retrieve my meat, my husband calling behind me, "Don't wound my daughter o. Because of meat, *kwa*."

I park in the cobbled drive and wind down the glass on each side. The smells of flowers hang in the air. Each building next to the main story looks like a fancy cake, and the story itself like a gateau.

"Your class teacher told me you fought again."

My daughter stares down her checked-blue school uniform, ironed by her dad to razor-edge lines. The Capri-Sonne packet lies crumpled beside her. "Yes, mummy. She said you look like King Kong in makeup. She and the other girls always say it." My daughter still has her baby voice. She will be seven in October. She does not raise her head.

I peer through the windshield at a woman tagging along behind her son as he drags her upstairs where my daughter's class (Primary Three) is, probably to show off a beloved teacher, or a watercolor painting. I do not take my eyes off mother and son hurrying delightfully up the stairs as I ask,

"So you beat her up?"

119

My daughter is silent.

"Unstrap your belt and come down."

Open Days fill me with *exciety*—a brittle blend of fear of the unknown and intrigue for the known. My daughter leads her class. She also fights like a monster in class. She once yanked off a classmate's hair-band and gave her a sound beating. The proprietor, a timorous church reverend behind stone-framed glasses, summoned me and tried to scare me.

"Alhaja. You are someone we highly respect; your contributions to this school are immense. But your daughter has been frequently accused of juvenile misdemeanor in this great and cultured citadel. We will not condone such delinquencies. We have an image to protect, and a God to give an account to. One more report from her class teacher and we may be forced to suspend her." He spoke in a rush, blinking as if his glasses were not enough protection from my eyes. He had blinked like that during the first PTA meeting I attended, when he suggested my daughter come to school with her hair covered only on Fridays, since Friday was Jumm'at, a Muslim day. He must have known he was trying to twist a rock around his finger; at home, we ourselves couldn't talk our daughter out of it. She says the other girls wear their Anglican rosaries every day, so she will wear her hijab every day.

I tilted forward, right over the piles of books and the quiet atlas in one corner of the table, and let him know. "This is a religious-run school. They steal my daughter's pocket money even if she straps her bag around her waist. And I don't think you have summoned their parents yet, because they are still taking my daughter's money. Where are these morals? Don't talk to me about suspension. *I*—"

I patted my chest "—should be the one talking about withdrawal. Fix the problems in your school and my daughter will have peace." Then I smiled my widest smile, leaned back, arranged my scarf-ends around my neck, and said, "Reverend, it's sunny outside; won't you serve me chilled Coke?"

He fled.

My daughter grabs her lunch box and climbs out. I let her walk round, tuck her arm through her bag-strap, and slip her hand into mine. Teachers and parents alike nod at us as we pass, some shouting greetings and rubbing my daughter's cheeks, their faces veiled with admiration, and I wonder which one of them had been there when my daughter's classmate called me "a King Kong on makeup".

OMOMIZIE

Crazies no dey write am for their number plates o. *Hian!* The okada man that brought me and my daughter here is definitely crazy. He has to be ment. No one can tell me he's not. Zipping like that through traffic! E remain small make e tuck me and my daughter under one Coca-Cola truck around that filling station. God go punish him for us. And no be im fault! If the man who calls himself my husband was not busy laying the bed with other women, what would a fine girl like me be doing flying okada? *Se* he would have saved enough money and bought me a small Hyundai that has A/C *je-e-je*? Ehh! He knows my kind of skin won't thrive under this crazy Nigerian sun, this one that they have now peeled away all the ozone layer with their stupid pollution. We all know he'd be cold dead first before he replaces my sunscreen creams. But he could just get me that car. How much is it? At least, it's not going to be as big as the Toyota he's "cruising town" and seducing those

121

toothpick-leg girls with—if that's what's scaring him. Nonsense! And he dared to call me to talk about food. Food! This early momo. He didn't eat at his *soyoyo*'s place? *Abi* na just to spread legs; they don't know how to cook? If that man tries me today, I will show him I'm a correct homebred Bini babe! I am here appearing for his child's Open Day and he's there talking about food. If he comes to this girl's school today, will his penis shrink? Talmabout "Darling, what did you make for me?" How about shit? Shit from my yansh! Big brown lumps scooped out of the water-closet bowl and placed in a dish for you! *Osinwin* man!

I *sha* trust my mother. "Mama Nurse". People said she looked frail, dainty, but all of us in our family knew she had loose bolts in her head. She was *vawulence* herself. May she rest in peace! She would have fried my husband's gbola, with the balls join, and given him to eat to teach him some manners!

Toh. I will come back to his matter later. I have a pressing issue I have to settle once and for all with them in this school. A particular demon of a child has been roughing up my child for some weeks now, and it just has to stop. What nonsense! Is it because my daughter looks delicate? So one emere child from nowhere will just assume she can bully her and go scot-free? *O paro!* Has she not heard of Edo girls before? We fly, man. We don't walk on the surface of earth anymore. What kind of a mother does she have anyway? Doesn't she see her child raving around like a market madwoman? Doesn't she see she is raising an angry child? Despite my mother's craze-head, she never taught us to fight unprovoked. Even when provoked, she raised us to handle the moment like a surgeon. We don't strike with a hammer when a fly perches on a man's scrotum. We don't. I trained Ibinabo well. She would not disgrace me publicly, unlike the other uncouth goat of a child. *Toh*. Today na today, no be another day. I will first see their class teacher to give him my daughter's last term report—he has an error he must rectify in it and I kept forgetting—and then let him know I am already getting pissed off about my daughter and her bully of a classmate.

I am standing in front of my daughter's classroom, waiting for her teacher whom the pupils I asked said was in the toilet, when a woman darts past me, almost running me over. She is huge! She has appeared in a swish of silk. She smells like imported wine. She is not beautiful, but she carries an aura that is more attractive than beauty. A man like my husband may not do as much as kiss her. But he will definitely nurse the idea of lifting her silk and seeing what is underneath it. That dog!

"Madam, please watch where you are going!" I call after her, but she has raced down the stairs towards a red Citroen parked in the drive. Ibinabo is still sucking on the stick sweet I bought her that morning before we hailed the deranged bike man. I glance down at her, then look away; she may not have an answer. I turn to peek at the expensively dressed Muslim woman. She must be a shareholder, or a supervisor. She can't be a parent—I've never seen her. Well, I could be wrong. I just brought my child here last term. Or maybe I wasn't paying that much attention. Whatever! She should not push me down just because she glows like American cream and has a car! All of una dey craze!

MEMUNAT

My daughter's Maths teacher needs me to give him my card. He wants to snap it and send my contact to his uncle

123

in Jos, a museum curator who often comes down to Edo to buy bronze heads imitations and ivory masks. "I saw your art pieces on Instagram and I must say they are *mag-ni-fi-cent*," he said, eyes sparkling, so I am back in my car, rifling through my glove compartment, where I suppose I have a number of cards for emergency customers. My husband will roast me if I find none; he says if everyone had half my level of incompetence, no one—not even he—would be gainfully employed. He's the manager at EmmaCorn Trust Bank and thinks the world rests on his shoulders. It doesn't stop him from farting under the covers when we are in bed. Or slurping his tea like his daughter does. I am still rummaging through the bric-a-brac when my hand knocks down a folded sheet of paper. I pick it up and stretch it out; the wrinkly surface does nothing to distort the too-familiar spidery penmanship. It is a photocopy of my mother's letter to her childhood crush and closest friend. I found it years ago, along with her diary, while sorting her house a day after we buried her in her family compound in Afuze. It astonished me to read the contents, how similar my mother's life and mine are and yet how hidden from each other, till death. I do not know how the letter got into my car, but I had been looking for it for ages. It's like a psychedelic drug; I go to it from time to time; I have sorely missed it.

Hello, Adesuwa,

It's been a while. You just went to nursing college and forgot me here. Not one letter have you sent. Is that how sweet Lagos is? Since you and your family moved, I've felt like a lone sandhouse. It's like the next draft will blow and scatter me all over the place. The other day, I trekked to

NITEL office to complain to the operators about our broken home phone. But you know how those people are. "We'll come and check, we'll come and check"—that was what they kept saying.

I am tired.

So I am doing what I hate most: writing a letter. Because—because I miss you.

Someone taps on my glass. I look up; it's one of the cleaners. "Thank you for the dress and shoes, ma," she says, genuflecting like a Yoruba woman.

"*Alhamdulillah,*" I say. Thank God. I smile back at her, nod and watch her go. She has the most beautiful nose I have ever seen on a human. When I touch myself on nights when my husband is too tired to touch me, I sometimes think of her, hold her face, her nose, in the nucleus of my mind, until my wetness pushes against my finger. It does not feel wrong; it never feels wrong. I return to the letter.

How is your mother? I miss her. The way she talks and all her body shakes. And her permanently hoarse voice. You know how— the few times we caught each other at the market or at the community borehole—we used to joke about her living in a church, shouting at God, praying for you so that you could become normal. I'm happy she now prays for better things, like peace of mind, like love. At least, I knew that before you guys left.

And her cooking! Ade! You and I know my mother can't boast of such delicious magic.

I miss you. I miss us. Do you remember playing in the rain in September, only our panties covering us, until my mother yelled at us and swore to pull our ears off? *Osanobua*, I feel a drop on my skin even as I write this. There were times we saw both the sun and the rain, and that was when the butterflies came out. My mother would say the tigress was giving birth and you would argue that it was more scientific than that. I would say it was God. God means "something you can't explain conclusively". You would disagree and say I was beginning to sound like your mother. Then we would hurry out to the backyard, perhaps to catch the mythical tigress pushing out her cub, or to watch God play with both rain and sun, like a child plays with art. We used to open the backyard door with an angry slap because it was always stuck. Do you remember all this?

I stop reading and lower my head to the steering wheel.

OMOMIZIE

Teacher Toilet is back. I am standing next to him, groping my handbag for Ibinabo's result.

"Where's the proprietor?" I ask him.

"He's not in school yet."

"I see. He will come here and meet me."

I pull out something.

He peers at the sheet in my hand. "Madam, don't tell me you didn't bring that result *again*? I am beginning to suspect that you are making up tales."

My hands drop to my sides. The paper I yanked out of my inner zip is not Ibinabo's result; it is the photostat of an old missive written by my mother. No, not to me. But to a friend, a lover, who did something unforgettable in her childhood. I carry it around like a shadow.

"Excuse me for a moment, please," I say to the man, who looks bewildered by the switch in my mood. I feel like salt soaked with water. "Ibinabo love, go downstairs and play with your mates. Mummy is coming, okay?" I dig my hand in my purse and give her a 50-naira bill. "If you want anything, use that at the school confectionery." I watch my daughter skip away as though she had anticipated the permission. I flash her teacher a faint smile. "Where's the toilet for women, please?"

He asks a tall girl to lead me and I trudge after her. I'm going to sprinkle water on my veins. I'm going to read, once again, the words that have become a second heart in my chest.

War can wait.

Hickey Hiqmat,

My Chori-Chori.

Do you still draw dots in the middle of your forehead with your mother's antimony? You fool. Bush fowl.

Vbee oye he? Sorry about the NITEL people wahala.

I am going to try and make this very brief. Nursing school in Lagos is quite mad. Lagos itself is a mad place. If you don't move fast, they will rob you of everything, your time, your clothes, your documents, your money, your food. In fact, they can steal you away completely from where you stand. *Eko wenjele!*

But I may go on and on, and miss my anatomy class. You have a way of getting me talking, loosening me up.

See, Hiqmat. First, I am sorry for not reaching out to you. I promise you, it's not because of what happened. Time has just become something else in this place. Do you know that I sometimes forget to brush my teeth and I go for my clinicals just like that! It is what living in Lagos does to you.

I must confess to you. A part of me is still mad at you. Do you know my parents, till today, do not know that I flushed out my insides? I simply told them I lost the child. They were dismayed. They worried that Eghosa would call off the engagement. I told them I was not a baby-making machine. Any man that would marry me must marry me for my whole self. I am not a womb. I am not a vagina.

Till today, they don't know Eghosa was not the man behind the pregnancy. Even Eghosa himself thinks he lost his own baby. They do not know that Amenaghawon, a mere miscreant of no pedigree, was the one who hung up my legs in his uncle's mechanic shop and drove himself into me while you stood by and watched.

Hiqmat. How could you? *I TRUSTED YOU.* It was your birthday, Hiqmat. I *had* to beg my mother to at least let me go give you the beads I made you. You shouldn't have spoiled it like that. You slipped something in my Fanta. You said we should walk down the road to go check on our sandhouses. We were on our way, singing the call-and-response songs from our elders' folktales. Then I slumped in front of Amenaghawon's mechanic shed. You had planned it so well.

I went through hell the morning after. How I got back home—till today—I don't know. I woke up feeling like someone scratched sandpaper all over my skin. I throbbed between my legs. It was nothing like your beautiful finger. I felt cut open. I ran a terrifying fever. I vomited everything my mother gave me, pills and food. She later bundled me to the clinic in Benin City, where the doctor told her what had happened to my body. My mother was distraught. She knew where I had been. My father threatened to send her packing, but she refused, my mother, she refused to talk. She kept our secret. She kept our dirty little secret.

Bangs on the toilet door—"Is anyone in there? Hello? Can't hear the water."

Someone has to go. I scoot down from the toilet lid and squeeze the door open. A slim woman, her hair worn in neat cornrows, walks past me, meeting my apologies with a quizzical smile. I walk away. She only peed, so when I hear her flush and come out, I return to my hideout, squat on the toilet lid, and fall on the paper again.

> And yet—*yet*—Hiqmat, my Chori-Chori, a side of me can't afford shutting you out. What we shared even before we kissed still lingers. No matter where I go, no matter whom I end up with, you and I are one. You are me, I am you. From generation to generation. So how can I be angry at myself?
>
> No.
>
> You were just being foolish. You thought you could redeem yourself in my father's eyes by making a penis guide me to normalcy. You thought you could redeem your family's image in everybody's eyes. You needn't have gone to that length to prove a moot point. What if I had died while flushing my womb with acid? What if I had perforated it, lost it entirely? I stuck my sister's hanger up into me, Hiqmat. What if I had ripped myself out? You taught me nothing, love. I had always recoiled from a man's body. When Eghosa touches me, he senses it. He senses that there will never be an easy chemistry between his body and mine. I only force myself to yield to him so that he won't think it has something to do with his

albinism. It is not new, has never been. I have felt like that long before you and I kissed. And I know both touches loosen you up, unlike me. But you shouldn't have forced me down that path with you, just to make me be like you. I would have loved you nonetheless. I would have loved you.

MEMUNAT

I lift my head. Through the thick glass of the Benz, the pupils running around in their checked blue look like light dancing on water. All around me, I see a greenish film. I rub my eyes to clear them. My daughter is crawling up a slide chute. Now, she's skidding down on her butt. Now, she's screeching, revealing her lower gap-teeth, revealing her dimples. She's holding a coffee-skinned girl of about her age and rubbing the girl's head, the way children do when apologizing. Soon, both of them are holding hands and trotting away from the swings, to the bouncing castle, to the hand bars, then back to the slides. A woman is standing in the verandah, watching my daughter slide down the facility, among other kids. I first noticed her when she came out from the direction of the bathrooms, wiping something from her eyes. She is tenaciously pretty, as if the many black moles and reddish freckles on her pale pink skin can't douse her effulgence. Her blond hair is pulled up tight in a bun. She is watching with a smile. The two girls are now sliding down at a single pace. I will get down soon and go see my daughter, but I have to finish what I started. I have never left my mother's letter halfway. Never.

Hmm. Enough dancing around the bush. I'm happy for you and your family. I hope your father is no longer angry with me. Does he still think I'm an evil spirit? Please, tell him there is nothing evil about me. There is nothing evil about my love for you. We once tried to bury it, you and I. We avoided each other and went for boys. My body could still handle it, but yours—yours couldn't.

I'm sorry. I'm so sorry, Ade. I should have taken the cue from you from our trials that you would always find boys rough and jagged and that they would close you up tightly. I thought Amenaghawon would help, since almost every girl in the community liked him for his rugged looks. I forgot that you are not "almost every girl". I am so very sorry. I know you said you forgave me, before you left. But I can't help feeling you still hate me. That you hate me for what happened. I also hate myself. I thought I was helping. I thought I would wriggle myself into your father's good books, after that night he caught us behind the water drum. He shone his torchlight in our direction, directly, premeditatedly, as if he had been waiting for that night to happen. We did not know he was coming. How could we have known and still done what we did? He was supposed to be sleeping, after that long day at his farm. He clicked on his torch *tukum* and caught us. Our naked legs tangled, my lips clinging to your nipple, my finger gliding between your thighs, my other hand kneading your breast. You were a poetess that night. You were chanting my name—*Hiqmat, Hiqmat*—and each rhythm guided my finger and tongue. I was already feeling the wetness surge outward and I think you just clutched my back and arched yours when the beam from your father's torch appeared and cast us apart.

You yourself know what I went through. He reported to my mother. The family elders blamed her for raising her girl like a prostitute; they said that my mother's upbringing of me was responsible for what happened. They said that was the problem with single mothers; that the lack of a man in a house turned the children into things that could not be recognized. They beat the hell out of me. My mother wept for weeks and wouldn't touch the *omisagwe* I made her. I was shattered. Your father forbade me coming to your house, forbade us seeing each other. Our playground became empty. Our sandhouses were abandoned. Butterflies became a rare phenomenon. Rainy days transformed into nightmares for me, and I avoided windows. Even your mother who used to smile at me and buy pomade for my hair quickly turned a red eye upon me each time I rode my bicycle past your house and dared to greet her. I was literally an outcast in my own land. Everybody said you were not like that, that I had initiated you into my spirit world. But how else could I tell the world I was not an *ogbanje*; how else could I prove to everyone that I could fix you back since I was the one who made you like that? That was why I did what I did. I did it and I hated myself even before I saw the tears and mucus on your face.

I hate myself.

"Sorry" won't mend things, but I am really sorry. We have moved from Ekpoma back to my mother's hometown. I will write my new address and landline on the envelope. Please, write back. Or call back.

We need to talk. I want us back. I hate missing you.

Your 'Indian' girl,

'Hickey' Hiqmat.

P.S.: I still keep the bead necklace. I will give it to my daughter—if I have any. It will be a token from her godmother. I wish I were worth being one for your child.

Splotches have started landing on the sheet, melting the black ink. I finger the necklace nestled beneath the neckline of my silk gown. What is wrong with me today? This is not my first time reading it. I had never cried over it before. *If the world were smaller and the fates benign, I would meet my mother's girlfriend's daughter.*

OMOMIZIE

The sweet-smelling woman has come to join me. She must be an Alhaja—I saw a glint of gold when she smiled her greetings at me. Perhaps she has a child here after all. Who cares? I am a little bored, but this girl is pretty. And I feel towards her a kinship akin to blood. It's as if I *know* her.

But I don't. I shouldn't. It's this instinct. My daughter looks uncertain around her. Perhaps she's even the one beating my girl up all the time. Today *sha*, I will settle it. Just let their proprietor arrive.

I unfold the letter again. I want to re-read the concluding lines slowly. My mother had grace, forget it. Mama Nurse. She may not have had all the happiness she wished for in her life, but she had grace. I won't ever forget that legacy left in those lines. It's like pressing on a clotted sore; I relish the sweet agony.

> I forgive you, Hiqmat. In this life and the next. *Oy'ese.*
>
> Yours forever,
>
> Adesuwa.
>
> P.S.: May you have a daughter, and may she be more determined about her life choices than you are.

I hope to meet this daughter someday, this daughter of whom my mother wrote.

THE OMNISCIENT

Neither woman knows what the other is thinking, or who the other one is. They simply keep their mothers' letters, press their foreheads to the dusty net and watch as their daughters sweep down the slides, swatting at each other's ponytail, shrieking and pretending to fall over.

GILBERT

I am not a tall man—my early crises have sucked out my flesh and stunted my legs, because God gave me cells that are shaped like a farmer's sickle—but yet Gilbert is shorter than I am. And perhaps that's why he is capable of a solidness, an unwaveringness, a groundedness that may never shake, or perhaps that's not why. But Gilbert is shorter than I am, and sometimes when he kisses me, my neck hurts from having to bend too much. He noticed one Friday evening in my father's house, in the lonely compound full of old undying flowers and crisp brown fallen-off leaves that crunch under our feet when we hold hands and walk around. We do this often, listening to our dreams and the echoes of our footfalls.

"Your legs move in unison," my sister, Bibi-Ire, had said when we visited her that afternoon at the hospital after the delivery of her boy. "You people didn't know? That's why I kept staring below your knees when you walked in. Now that you're leaving, they are still moving in the same procession. *Na wa* for you two. *Kukuma* restrict my airflow *na*."

Gilbert had laughed, a delirious laughter ringing with the glee that comes with being congratulated for something grand achieved, and I had kept my lips bashfully sealed, too aware that what Gilbert and I share had already started showing on our legs. Gilbert calls it "discomfort". That Friday evening, while he kissed me goodbye on the desolate stairs of my father's porch, I had to lean my neck down even more, since he was standing at the bottom of the stairs, not close to me as usual. I must have grimaced, or let out a grunt, because he opened his eyes, narrowed them, and disconnected from our lips.

"You don't feel comfortable?"

I looked down and nodded, afraid to watch his eyes, afraid that I had hurt his feelings. But he burst out laughing.

"Why didn't you just say so?"

I smiled and looked away. He always said I was too shy for a Top, that I would make a submissive husband. It was one of his few stellar jokes that were able to pry my stiff lips apart in a loud gurgle of laughter. I hoped he would not crack the joke now, nor say something similar; I didn't want to laugh and ruin the moment building in my chest. *I love kissing you, I just don't know how to*—I wanted to say. *And I'm too scared to let you teach me 'cause I know you'll go wild on me. And I will do things I've never done before. Things I've always wanted to do.* The evening wore itself on me like a fridge. The moon sliced through the sun-bereft clouds, like a silver scythe, but it was pale. I could hear the prelude of cicadas.

"Do you miss your father?"

I was thrown by the suddenness of the question. "What?"

He pulled gently on my hand so that I glided down the stairs, with the sensation of a groom walking into the waiting arms of his intended, until I stood on the same level as he. He came up to my shoulder.

"Do you miss Dad?"

"Yes." I felt the insides of my eyes burn. "Yes, I do."

137

He wrapped his hands around himself, from the cold I think.

"Do you regret coming out to him?"

"It wasn't my coming out to him that killed him." I was grateful that he didn't squeeze my hand, or have that silly, inconsolable furrow of sorrow that people have on when they speak of my father's death, as though he had been their own father rather than mine.

"Moonbeam, I know." Gilbert's tone was solacing, but not patronizing. I hated myself for expecting him to gloat.

He comes from a lineage of infamous prudes: a cousin who once screeched in genuine horror when a girl hawker used her bare hand to pack peeled oranges for them at Balogun market; a mother who doesn't look at her housemaids while giving them instructions; a grandmother who was once said to have wiped her foot on the back of a houseboy who spilled hot tea on her leg; a father who hates sharing the roads of Lagos with "common truck drivers and Keke three-wheelers", and so only flies his private jet for anything that takes him out into the Mainland; a successful actress aunt who thinks it is horribly low-class to respond to people's encomiums on Twitter, follow people back on Instagram and reply comments from fans on Facebook.

Each time Gilbert speaks of his family, and of their insouciant response to his coming out as homosexual, he uses that same gently comforting tone, as if he fully understands how different it was for me, how my mother had kicked me out when I came out, and I had had to seek refuge in my father's abandoned house. How I was never a self-assured Aje-butter whose harsh life realities were at least numbed by the luxuries of indulgent, impersonal family ties. How it is only Bibi out of my five siblings that does not look at me like I have elephantiasis between my legs. When Gilbert speaks of me and my family, he is careful not to sound excessively pitiful.

"I never said it was you coming out to him that killed him. He had angina and I know his doctors said he didn't have much longer to live." Gilbert placed his hands over my ears, his fingers resting lightly on my glasses' frames, a cryptic gesture he loved, still loves, making. "But do you wish you hadn't told him about you?"

"I would have hated it more if he had died without knowing who I am. I could never have forgiven myself."

Gilbert pressed his forehead against mine. Every last Friday of the month, we go round to the back of my father's house, to the marble grave that holds my father, and we kneel by it and pray. I don't go first; I always kneel at the same time with Gilbert, holding his hand and talking to my father. The Friday of this story was the penultimate. It seemed funny, in a macabre way, how we had attended a birth this Friday and how, the following Friday, we would be paying a visit to the grave, a constant requiem to the dead. Gilbert had offered to buy the flowers this month.

"Why did you say 'babies are so clueless' while holding your nephew at the hospital?" he asked me, foreheads stapled.

I moved my tongue in my mouth so it would become moistened, so that it would not cling to the roof of my mouth and hold the words that I wanted to say. "Because babies don't know how they were born."

He hummed shortly, leaned back and gazed at me for so long I thought he had fallen asleep standing. I peered at him to make sure, but his eyes (the part of his body that drives me crazy the most) were twinkling under that gray bowler hat he so religiously wears. His dreadlocks hung down like strips of twined jet-black wool. His hands still cupped my ears.

"Were you thinking just that, Olu, or were you thinking about us having babies?"

"I was thinking both," I said, startled by the ease of my speech.

It was the same way it had been easy with Mr Oputa, the CEO at the modeling agency in Ikeja. Mr Oputa whose office gleamed and hummed and blew petal scents softly. Mr Oputa who had a toothpick permanently stuck in his mouth, dangling over his lip. Mr Oputa who wore a blue jacket and an air of amorality, and played with his swivel chair. He had gone through my credentials and given me a wink that confused me where I sat. He asked me if I had ever runway-modeled for any company. While I was still speaking, he pushed himself up, went round the table, didn't stop, went round me, behind me, and touched the nape of my neck lightly, so lightly that I was surprised in retrospect to realize that all of his five fingers had rested on my skin. I felt my hair rise. I jerked around and slapped his hand down. He stepped back, stunned.

"Is this the way you touch everyone who comes in here, as if you own them, or am I just different?" I asked him. "I'm here for detached aesthetics. I want to show the unusual beauty of my body to the world as an exclusive art, not to you. This is disappointing. I was warned but I thought it was ridiculous and untrue. Is this how you grope boys who come for an engagement? Too bad. You should be ashamed of yourself, sir."

I got up, snatched up my papers, and left his fragrant-air office, mourning my transport fare, feeling the weight of his hand on me, feeling like I should spit. I wandered around, too self-conscious to stay put. Finally, as the sun fell and twilight shielded me, I took the *molue* ride back home, sitting at the very back, looking out the window at the night market women chattering and raising tin lamps, watching the amber street lights zebra-line the skin of my arm, wondering if the voice that had uttered those words back inside the modeling agency truly belonged to me. That night, in the bathroom, I scrubbed my neck with extra vigor. When I told Gilbert about it, he was even angrier. The contact lens in his eyes flashed. "*That* was lecherous! Why are there so many perverts out there? That was how my sister Bedi's husband's cousin was told to lift her skirt in the manager's office before they could hire her as PR. Imagine! I know everybody in this country is horny but people's bodies are not your property!" I looked at the extra redness of Gilbert's eyes and realized that I had slapped off Mr Oputa's hand not because I was terrified of sex but simply because it was annoying. It *was* annoying.

Gilbert blew on my glasses to call me back. A small mist appeared. He gripped my ears, gently, so gently I imagined his fingers as feathers, before he said, "But we can have babies, Olu. We can have as many babies as we want."

"I know." I avoided his eyes again, this time sure that I had hurt him, if just a little. I hated the way I was beginning to sound. "I just... Actually, it's not about us having babies or not. I really don't care whether we have kids or not; that's obviously not why I'm with you. When I held my nephew's small warm body in that ward and peered at his closed eyes, I realized how much we already are at birth, and how so much more it seems we grow up to be, and how both of these things happen without our permission the moment we start becoming aware of our world and our lives start reading like time."

He stared at me. I wanted to remove his hat and use it to cover my face. In 2016, when we first met in Aba where I had gone for a Book Reading, and he asked for my WhatsApp digits and I said I didn't have WhatsApp on my phone and he asked for my Facebook ID and I admitted I didn't have an account, he had given me that same stare, as if I was a wrapped object he suddenly had a mission to unravel. He had said, "I would ask you for your Yellow App details but I have a feeling you would say 'What is a Yellow App?' "

"What is a Yellow App?" I had asked anyway, before I realized I shouldn't, before we laughed and I laughed my mobile number into his phone. That night, he texted me a string of disconnected sentences, as if he worried that he would scare me off any which way so he had better just get on with it:

"You have a nice laugh. I'm Bottom in bed.

You're effeminate and it's cute.

My pastor thinks I should not lock my hair anymore, unlike what he and I first agreed on. He said half of his congregation would not understand, and I see his point."

He said now, in a similar pattern. "You have a dope point there. I want to be a baby again. I promise I would start drawing my rainbow colors earlier on every wall in our house rather than spend so much time standing in my closet."

I stared up into the trees. They were looming silhouettes in the gloaming that had descended on both of us, with its early January breeze. Through their dark foliage, the new moon was sharpening, a silver sliver in a sun-shorn sky. A dream. I wanted to ask Gilbert to sing me a song, or take a picture of me, or read me a poem. I wanted the stars to come out.

"What is it? What's making you smile?" He hooked his arms around my shoulders now, and my temples felt the vast empty space of loss. There was a taunting tilt to his lips that accentuated his beautiful, beautiful jaw. I looked away, wanting to scold the abrupt swelling in my trousers. He drew back, a sharp movement, and gasped. I wanted to vanish through the floor.

"Hey, I feel tall." His face was split open in childlike delight.

"You do?" I gaped, thrown off-balance again.

"Yes! See." He kissed me, and the surprise that I hadn't even needed to move my head at all made me lose my words altogether. "See?" His lips meshed with mine again; this time, he took longer. "See?" He kissed me again.

I giggled, drunk on the magical wonder of it all. "You must have tiptoed, you cheat. Don't take this as an excuse to continue kissing me *o*."

He laughed and pulled me close. I buried my nose in his chest. He smelled of wine and Coconuts biscuits and an early rain. He smelled of strength. I drew my hands around his shoulders and slowly slid them down to the small of his back, to his firm waist, and kept them there.

I cook reinvented dishes every week and wonder if anyone really wants to eat them. Just the week before,

Gilbert opened an Instagram account for me, and now I have to upload my cuisines on my Instagram page, watermarked and mouthwateringly enhanced. Customers say they taste even better than they look; while reading feedback, I grin at my catering school certificate that sits pretty on my bedside desk. Gilbert has offered to drop home deliveries with his scooter, while I supervise the larger event bookings. It surprises me, the ready and relentless swiftness with which he makes the trips, laughing about what a customer had said about the food, helping to count and sort the money while Sia yodeled in the background, and then rushing back again to his clothing complex in Festac, where his small staff will have collected materials from the middle-class socialites who keep pouring in. Gilbert's workers are startlingly swift. Before Gilbert knows what's happening, they will have fixed diagrams of required styles on CorelDraw, run measurements and started work on the machines. Gilbert marches around with his phone set to Instagram Live, fingering his white ivory choker, teasing them with sneak selfies and shots—"Hey, Anita, you look like Viola Davis threading that thing"; "Bona, I'm totally sending this to your girlfriend, I bet she has never seen you look this committed"—or without his phone—"You look tired, Mabel. Get up and go home. Take this and take an Uber. Don't worry, you can close earlier today, I'll fix this. Now don't be stubborn"; "Chidi, were you thinking of your sugar mummy when you cut that bust? *Biko*, check the customer's stats again o, we can't afford careless lapses".

Gilbert takes life like his very own creation, as if he were the one responsible for its rises and falls. It's the same stick-to-itiveness on his face when we visit orphanages in April (for Easter) and then in December (for Christmas). He wastes no stride; he walks pointedly in front of the caregivers, his silver anklet glittering, double-checking, interviewing some of the children personally, going back to the owner's office to sign the donations records, and saying a firm "No" when a photographer comes to ask us to join the gathered children for media shots.

When my hypoxemic attacks come every other fortnight, benign and languorous, Gilbert calls his private doctor and she comes to my father's abandoned house with a full oxygen kit that she barely exhausts. He emphasizes that I will have to rest, as if he is not sure I have heard the doctor correctly. Then he touches me, briefly, just below my belly button. I keep thinking of our first time, how it will be. It is something I think of only because I think he thinks of it, too. I am conscious of failing myself before him—in any manner. He says we will employ hands soon, "to divide the weight"—as he puts it. He is worried that I will keep having crises and have to spend all my net on drugs, albeit I tell him often that—but for the constant painful throbbing of my inner thighs and the exhaustion that roils within my chest region after cooking—I am fine. And it's true. I *am* fine. I may always have reasons to withdraw into my shell, to reduce my volumes, to jump less exultantly. But I have Gilbert.

In my father's compound, I leaned closer into his embrace, as if I needed to melt into him, and time watched us quietly, broken only by the chirping of the cicadas, and the cooing of homebound doves. When we pulled apart, hands connecting, I looked down and realized that I was standing like he, my legs placed firmly on the cobbled floor, unwavering, grounded, solid. I could weather any storm. I could win anything.

THE BANISHMENT

You are trembling by the threshold of the shrine. The night holds the rain up, but its wind spreads the moisture over your back. Behind you, out in the yard, your mother is still wailing, and your father's other wives are still holding her down. A huddle of elders stands there, too, murmuring, their tones grave. You don't see them when you look back. The moon is full, but the swollen rain clouds have eclipsed it. Vision has now become like peering into your mother's pots, into which she dips taffeta cloths for dyeing every day of the week so she can sell them at Oja-Oba. *Iya Alaro*. Perhaps after tonight, she will never sell dyed cloth again, never show her face again before people. In the shrine, a lone oil lamp flickers and casts half-light on the grim faces standing around. The Oluwo's voice comes in echoes, loud echoes, but you don't hear them. You are staring at Lakiitan. At least, in the penumbra, you *can* see him. He is flattened at the far end of the hut, chewing his lower lip as usual, the red-earth wall behind him dark with shadows. The low flame makes him look like an apparition. You imagine walking into his mind to see if he is also afraid of the unknown, if the fear crumpling your insides is also crumpling his insides.

The floor of the shrine, a dank stretch underfoot, leaves your soles bloodless. The Oluwo is in white and chanting incantations—you can now hear him clearly—clattering his seeds-gourd, calling on the witches of the earth, invoking the gods of the dome between heaven and earth who preside over abominations, and asking them what exactly should be the penalty for you and Lakiitan, for doing what nobody has ever done before. *What nobody has ever done before.* The expression has clamped its teeth into the skin of your ears; everybody has been using it.

"Why did you do what nobody has ever done before? Why? Since when had you been nursing that idea?" your mother had asked, peering into your eyes as if to aspirate the truth from there. The truth that would be a lie. "You know how things are in your father's house. You know that my enemies in this house have been waiting to laugh at me. *Omo mi*, talk to me. *Ba mi s'oro.* Just say one word." She clasped your shoulders and shook. "*Ogunna kansoso, eyin ookan!* You won't say a word to why you have let the enemy get you. You won't talk to me. You have put me in disgrace!" She wept, disconsolate and disheveled as the whole Dasofolu village trooped to the chief priest's compound earlier in the day, the sun a sinking, burnished bowl in the sky. You and Lakiitan were walled-in in the middle of the two stalwart hunters who found you in the river, where you had bent over behind Lakiitan, while he moaned and wriggled his jiggly buttocks against your rock-hard abs, just before the sky fell on your heads.

Your father's words were not much different. They return to you now, with the wind. "I have always known that you are not my son," he said, a little too quietly, a little too slowly. And you almost believed you had broken his heart, and you hated yourself, and you hated him for making you hate yourself. "No son from my loins would be caught committing *eewo* with another boy." His voice rose. "No son of mine! *Eewo!*" He spat. "And in the Ojuna river, too! You found nowhere else for your evil act; it had to be the river the whole village worships." He covered his eyes. "How do

147

you want my fathers who bore offerings to that river and danced to praise it through their lifetime to be looking at me right now? I confirm today that your mother brought a bastard to my compound. I felt it from the day you ran away from a snake that you should have killed with an ordinary stone." He rocked his head. "It is just unfortunate that everybody has been seeing you as my *arole*. The one on whose shoulders I will crest my name, and the names of my forebears. *Agbo'le* Kutuje. But you have done a foreign thing; you can't be my blood. You have brought shame on my head."

You accepted it, calmly, that you had brought shame on his head. Is it not the duty of first sons, of any type of children at all, to bring shame on their parents' heads, simply by living alternate lives from what their parents have expected and, sometimes, even planned? Only he had been permitted to come into the communion hut with the Oluwo, while the clouds congealed above; others had been barred by the Oluwo's acolytes.

The Oluwo has stopped chanting. He pats down the dog-ears of his white cap. He levels your father with a piercing gaze.

"My fathers have spoken. My mothers, too, have said their own."

Your father hangs his head as if hiding from another calamity hurtling towards his reputation. "What did they say?"

"A firewood that is not useful in making fire for cooking has its final abode behind the hearth."

"Oluwo. It is you elders that also say no word can be big enough to require a knife to cut it. Say it to me exactly how it is. Stop speaking in parables."

The Oluwo takes a long time to reply. He strokes his amulet as if in a procedural rapprochement. You try to catch Lakiitan's face again. But he has looked away. You catch, instead, the impenetrable visage of the village idol in the corner, and the fresh animal skulls lolling against the wall, shedding blood and matted with feathers. A row of calabashes, containing things you cannot see, sits at the base of the muddy wall. The shrine heaves with the spirits of the dead and of the super-living. Inside this shrine, especially during the quondam times of intra-tribal war, the fate of Dasofolu's enemies has been negotiated and decided. The Dasofolu idol is particularly renowned for redirecting and drowning these battle-bearing foes in Ojuna, to protect its people. Thereafter, it refreshes the Ojuna waters. With impartial—if not more heavy-handed—ardor, Dasofolu's sons and daughters who have erred in the past have also been judged: adulterers stricken by lightning during a dry day, thieves struck with leprosy and elephantiasis, murderers bursting into curling maggots for months before they eventually die. You lock your hands behind your head. Perhaps the idol would swell your stomach, distend your scrotum, whiten the skin of your hands and legs. You and Lakiitan. You suddenly go still, very still.

The Oluwo clears his throat. "*L'ooto ni*. We do not die on the exact spot we stand while talking. The water jar has broken and its content spilled on the bare floor. Know this, Nikawo. It is not I that speak; it is the oracle that has pronounced it." He glances towards the glowing flame as though to call it a witness. He raises his eyes. "He shall be banished."

149

"Oluwo!" your father shouts.

"There is no going back, there is only going forward. *Tuoo!*" The Oluwo's spit lands like a hailstone. "The Devil has spoken. When the spittle falls on the ground, it does not find its way into the mouth again." His smile faces the light, a slash of dull orange in a face that looks bloated with glee. "The gods of this land are in their benevolent mood tonight, Tadenikawo. You should thank your *ori*. You should be thankful that they did not ask for your son's blood to be spilled to appease them and cleanse the land of this great impurity."

"Do not call him my son!"

You catch the Oluwo simpering. "Whose is he, then?"

Your father glares at Lakiitan. "What shall be done to the cripple?"

"The cripple is an *orisa*. A deity. He has been defiled. He is the victim here. Don't worry about him. I will keep him here for three moons. He will undergo some rites. And then he will be purged of all impurities."

"Nothing for my... the other boy? No animal sacrifices? Even human?"

"Nothing."

"His mother can dance. She can dance in the market. She can cross seven hills and—"

Laughter cracks through the night air. You start to shake again because, somehow, the Oluwo laughing just when your mother was mentioned rakes long lines down your nerves.

"Tadenikawo!" he says, flexing his eyes at your father, adjusting the shawl draped over his shoulder. "*Agbalagba kii*

150

se langba-langba! You are an adult, born into the arms of this village, and you know the way things are done. You know our gods. You know our traditions. You know your son is a reprobate of the land. Nothing can undo what he did. Except he is expelled from the land he defecated on."

"And nothing can chase out the evil spirit inside him?"

"You think I didn't ask the noisemakers of the night that question? You think I didn't consult the ones who drink from human skulls on it? I would prescribe goats, rams and yams. But I just want to eat. I would ask you to bring seven yards of white cloth. But I just want to make another *agbada*. No solution was revealed to me. Nothing can reverse this pronouncement. He is banished."

The world inside the hut pauses. Your father shakes his head.

"This is unfair."

"When something bigger than the barn is dug up, we sell the farm. We do not know the way of the gods. We cannot know. So we do not search, nor question them."

"But you claim to speak with them all the time!"

"What do you mean?" The Oluwo's eyes harden. "It is communing, son, communing. Communing is listening while the gods rumble like thunder!" He jiggles the staff in his hand, which rattles with a hundred castanet seeds, and suddenly points it in your direction. "You! You took advantage of his condition!"

"No." You want to cry. You want to lunge forward, grab and break his staff, kick down those effigies, smash those calabashes.

"You forced your way into him!" The Oluwo's words echo.

"No! Stop!"

"He didn't rape me! I seduced him!" Lakiitan makes as if to get up.

"Shut up! Or the gods will cast you out with him!"

And thus the priest's acolytes lead you out, a forked stake hooking your nape, into the forest. Your mother wails and wails. Her world has come unraveled. Her enemies have seen her end.

•••

The rain has finally begun—piney darts on the back of your neck, on your back, on your arms. You are shivering. The moon follows you, a guide for your ostracization. As a child, you had listened as your father gathered up all the children in the household and told them how the moon got a scar on its face and how that scar represented a man lifting his hand and hitting his wife for being disobedient and disrespectful. You gaze up at it now. The scar is buried in a watery film because of the rain, so you think it is not a man beating his wife; it is two people standing in a river, bent over, moving, rocking each other slowly, discovering grave truths about body and life. Your eyes stream; you drink from the sky. The forest does not mock you, and you are grateful to it. It parts and parts, makes room for your blind penetrations and assuages you with an envelopment of peace. It is not evil at all. Perhaps tomorrow, when the rain stops, anytime it stops, you will look to the east and find Osumare, the rainbow deity, the guiding god, stretching its hip across the sky. And it will lead you to where you will go and begin your life as yours to live, anew. You are suddenly filled with a cracked joy. Evil is not everywhere. It is only that place peopled with black-hearted humans that is nefarious. It is that place where they never talk about the great Osumare among the Dasofolu pantheon. It is in that same place where Lakiitan, your first love, will have to live on, without you.

You have always found the gods funny. You didn't ask to be born at all, let alone this way. You have never held the thought of a naked girl in your dreams. You have always avoided the girls who pranced around you during Erebe dance evenings in the village square, pushing their barely covered breasts at your mouth, or who cavorted too close, deliberately close, in the river while you swam. You avoided them, not because you were protecting your virginity as the arole of the Kutuje clan, but because you were repulsed by them. You didn't plan it, the epiphany in the river. It was deserted, at a time when farmers were bent over in their farms, cultivating and making ridges, when palmwine tappers were tapping their second round of gourds, when the women who washed in the dawn had long gone. You had prepared your sling as usual and taken your yam and palm oil breakfast, and were on your way to the bush close to the outskirts to see how many games the trap you had set on the path the evening before had caught. But you needed a swim first. Your underarms were slick. Your back itched. You untied your wrapper, hung it on a branch, removed your rubber slippers, and waded into the river, feeling giddy with blithe unreality. Anybody could have appeared and seen you. The water lapped against you, against the lump of you that had never known a girl's body. Or anybody's body. You daydreamed and stroked gently in the water. When you thought you should stop fooling about and pull out, a limping figure emerged, a lost look in his cross-eyes, crutches under his arms.

Lakiitan.

You knew him long before he showed up. He was Balogun's son, his lastborn by his second wife. He barely left his father's courtyard. You would see him sitting inside what you assumed to be his mother's hut, holding his wooden flute, his misaligned eyes shining through the low eaves. You didn't know about his limping until that day. You had heard that he was not just a talented singer but also a skilled swimmer, even if people whispered innuendoes behind him—when he sang on the market square or during festivals—that his legendary ugliness was too desecrating for the waters of the great Ojuna river. So you asked him to enter the water. He laid aside his crutches and obliged you. Or rather obliged himself, as you later realized, because as he sang about the tortoise and his clever wiles, and you felt yourself rise and swell under the water, and drifted away and away from him to lose the turgidity, he stroked closer and closer to you, until only the sharp water reeds were left for you to escape to. So you stopped, and he bobbed up to you, until your legs in the water touched his, his deadened ones. You wondered, illogically, if he felt anything from the contact. He grinned, still singing, then stopped, and turned, turned, until his barely clad derriere covered your furiously pulsing groin. When you groaned and set your beast free and instinctively rubbed it in-between his buttocks for long seconds to soften the way, and then finally eased it in, he did not refuse. He merely chewed his lips and closed his eyes.

You thought of asking him if there was any pain. But you couldn't say a thing. It was as if what was going on

154

needed no spoken words. It was when you were inside him, moving, so raw, so warm, so tight, that he finally started mumbling to you about how he had the body of a man but he had never felt like a man. It had always felt as if there was a gap between his mind and his body. You heard him clearly, even in the din rushing to your tip. You unlocked that door of your soul, the door that had always kept you from transcending your dreams, and you poured yourself out. Then the hunter who saw you first appeared. He yelped for his mate to come quickly and see what nobody had ever seen. It was that moment you knew that the sky over your head would change, that you should have at least told your mother about your forbidden dreams. It has a dark, zany tone to it: the first time you let your dreams spread in the water, the first time you poked yourself into a house and found it was home, is home and will always be, immediately after you broke that virginity you'd always held like a title, you have to pay for it. Heavily. You have loved him from that moment. But it wouldn't matter to anyone who heard. When does love become an abomination? When it expresses its lust? When this lust dares to be different, unfamiliar?

Howling winds are your answer; they gust against your light frame, taking advantage of your twisted, hollow insides, bringing nausea to your throat and deafness to your ears. The forest has hardened towards you, become arcane and alien. A new blindness is spreading over your eyes, infernal and internal, not from the gloom of the forest but from within you. You are surprised that you are not stopping. It is like a force is at your back, driving you, propelling you. You stumble over outgrowths and snag your face on thorny branches. But for the lightning that sets itself upon the forest through the overhanging foliage, you would have run into a ditch, too. You follow the frenetic flashes and totter around it, tilting to the edge of the forest where you think it is safer to tread. You don't know whether you are crying or it is the rain, but your eyes are stinging. Trees are crashing all around you, tired boles succumbing to the sound-waves bellowing from above. Strange flights are happening around you, the beating of wings, the panic of beaks, the shrieks of creatures whose homes have just fallen apart. In the commotion—and in the illumination from above—you find a disemboweled tree trunk. You don't know the name of the tree. In your blindness, you choose it for shelter. A startled python scrambles out. You go into transfixion. It glares at you to see if you are indeed an awkward branch. Its enormous head hisses and twists around your face. You do not move a muscle; you try not to think of your mother; you also hold your breath, willing your chest region not to glide. You imagine the snake swallowing you whole. Is this how people die? Is this how scandalized gods kill offenders? A soldier ant is crawling around in-between your thighs. It will bite you and you will move and the snake will strike. TheGulp you head-first. Smash your skull. The musty breath of the beast fans your face and shoulders steadily. Then it slithers away, crushing undergrowth in its wake, and you collapse into the hollow of the tree, where your deafness and blindness increase.

You are alive, drenched to the skin, and it's a miracle.

•••

The soldier ant bites you and you yelp awake. The storm has ceased; only the *drip-drip* from the foliage still lands on your bare back, tauntingly, like stones. You can see the first faint stirrings of the sun when you look up. Your neck aches. Your arms and feet throb. Your back is stiff. You step out of the tree trunk and stagger towards the light. The forest path feels mushy underfoot, as if all you need to sink through to a beyond unknown is to tighten your calves and apply pressure on your soles. A bird caws, unseen. A noise behind you stops you in your tracks; a twig just got knocked. With something that sounded like a plank.

"Akanni!"

You whirl around, your heart catching, because you recognize the voice. It is the voice from the river. It is the voice on moonlit nights. It is the voice in your heart.

It is him, quite all right. It is him.

How did he manage to escape the Oluwo's hut, and all those people? He is coming to you, limping towards you; he is with only one of his crutches. In his other hand, he holds something you cannot see yet.

"Lakiitan!"

"Akanni!"

He traipses over an outgrowth, and hits another twig, lumbering forwards, his crutch giving way.

"Lakiitan, wait! *Duro! O ma subu!* You'll fall!"

But Lakiitan is being impelled by invisible drums. The sky shines on him. He leaps, just in time, rising high into space and landing on one of his dead legs. The puddle from last night's downpour parts around his lifeless foot, a concentric clearing, a triumph, a prophecy. Something you have glimpsed in it makes you look up sharply, a band of layered colors, and it is true when you look up: Osumare is in the sky, with its motherly hip. You open your mouth to talk, but speech has run with the wind. Lakiitan lands in your outstretched arms. Just in time. You notice the band of tiny bones around his arm, and gasp.

"What are you doing?" you ask him.

He holds up the object in his hand, like an answer. "I grabbed a horn in the shrine and threatened to cut my throat with it if they touched me. I was shrieking. Your father ran out and blocked the entrance against the acolytes. I don't know why he did that. I asked for the Oluwo's amulet and he gave it to me. I asked for it like it would be a parting blessing. It's in my pocket. But this—this is yours."

He places the object in your palm. The necklet sits curled on your skin. You close your fingers around it and feel the new weight in your throat. A keepsake. Your mother picked a silk thread and strung it with beads on the night she pushed you out. She held you and called you "Akanni, Odumaresinaayomi," for you had opened up her womb and stopped the mouths that called her barren. "Your mother caught up with me in the woods and removed this from around her neck. She said no matter what happened to me, it must get to you. She said it was hers, for real, but the things she will remember are inside her and not around her neck. That you must have this so you can always be her son."

You watch him work his mouth for a while. His chewing has taken on a new vehemence, as if he's fighting tears. You are wondering what he will do if you place your lips around that mouth when he says, with all the passion in his small, frail body, "I am coming with you. My father saw what happened and has sent his dogs after me. He has threatened to lock me up for good. Even if he didn't, I made my decision in that shrine." He holds your eyes squarely. "I don't care where you go, whether it's the hills of Ibadan or the mountains of Osun. I'm coming with you. I don't live here anymore anyway."

You finally kiss him, a gentle pull of his lower lip, and then his upper. He shuts his eyes and a tear trails down his temple, and you also want to cry.

The sharp bark of a dog comes from the innards of the forest, too close, too bloodthirsty. You jerk up your head. The Balogun and the priest! You pick Lakiitan up from the forest floor; you leave the crutch behind because there is no extra time and no extra arm space. And, like a demon let loose, you run.

WHEN WE STOP

Ian checked his iPhone too often. The waiters glided past him in their tall hats, nodding respectfully at him, serving him bemused smiles. They shouldn't be wondering what a white immigrant was doing in an esoteric Lagos Island restaurant, but they were. Perhaps it was his demeanor, the way he seemed unable to sit still, looking antsily around, sitting alone at a table grandly set for two—a table replete with candles, bottled roses and "Happy 32nd Anniversary to Us, Babe" cards. But Ian refused to let his eyes linger on them and their unshielded curiosity. A medley of flavors assailed his nostrils, yet he sat, waiting for that one smell, that smell stronger than any aroma from any intercontinental kitchen in the world: Jackson's smell. Did he forget? But he had texted him! He had texted him that morning after they kissed goodbye in the garage and went to their separate work offices. The text had been quippy and drippy.

"Hey, Babe. What do you say to a serious business meeting at El Classico Kitchens, say, later in the day, around 7pm? Hold the paperweight; there will be one there, right where I'm sitting. Big one."

Even though Jackson did not text back, he had assumed he would have smiled. Smiled and probably just chucked the phone in his drawer and ordered his personal assistant to grab his executive portmanteau for yet another board meeting.

Ian shook his head, his heart lurching. The clock digits on his iPhone read "7.07". He zippered his fingers together and started cracking his knuckles, the same way he had done nearly two scores ago after he and Jackson, newly engaged at the time, held hands and bowed their heads solemnly before Jackson's uncle, Uncle Nwabunike, Jackson's only surviving adult male relative, and came out. The man had not flipped like Nigerians should flip, or like Ian had imagined Nigerians would flip. Instead, he had regarded them with an unprotesting, farsighted lugubriousness. Perhaps there was something forgivable about Jackson's ancestry, that biracial bloodline that Nigerians ignorantly called "half-caste"—his mother an inoffensive Indian American and his father the illustrious son of an Enugu farmer—that made Jackson's uncle say that surreal February afternoon, with a sympathetic shrug, "*O dimma.* What can I say? Sopuruchukwu has never toed the line of our ancestors anyway, right from childhood. It's only expected that he would want to slap our forebears in the face like this, so who am I to stop him?" Then he said something in Igbo, in grave tones, that Ian failed to catch and that he knew Jackson, who cared less about his cultural identities, had also failed to catch. It worried him slightly, but Jackson was already dragging him out into the flower-choked yard, and kissing him. "Let's get married!" he said, with a girlish laugh, as if he had been joking.

And now here they were: riotously and joyfully married for thirty-two years, and still counting. It was not a joke after all. He would have married him anyway, even if his uncle had foamed at the mouth.

"Should I call him?" he whispered to the little boy sitting at the next table, alone, while his parents took excited selfies by the gaudy floral alcove. The boy raised one

161

eyebrow and Ian said, "Oops, sorry." He poured himself a splash of Senõr and left it on the table undrunk. The revolving doors eased open and a couple walked in, hand-in-hand, dressed like the Fulani people in his Anthropology research books, the same ones in his new manuscript, due for publishing in October. It would be his fifth bestseller. He fidgeted with the clear bowl of rose petals in front of him. It was all he could do not to get up and pace around.

Finally, just when he picked his phone to ruin procedure and dial his husband's number, the door soughed open again, and that scent—that heady scent of memories, of many years steeped in challenges and victories and rebirth—came to him like the word of God:

Jackson.

•••

They hugged and kissed, and everybody (even the couple with their kid at the next table) minded their business. Ian pulled out the chair on the other side of the table. He wondered what had happened to Nigerians. They must have assumed they were both Americans and, since Americans didn't carry the shadow of mores, therefore were exculpable. Jackson apologized. There had been ridiculous backlogs at the office. Plus, there was that contract he had been targeting for ages.

"Those Chinese think I came back to oversee my father's estate firm with kid gloves on my hands. It's absolutely preposterous. What sort of bid was that? Telling me it was a competitive pitch and they were breaking protocol by coming to me privately. Nonsense! You need to have heard the market figure they kept pushing into my face. Almost made me speak an Igbo curse."

Ian laughed. It was easy to laugh now that Jackson was standing right in front of him. Jackson was like an asset that enchanted him, a kind of elixir. He must always be around. He gestured towards the seat he had drawn out.

"I'll sit later, I need to feel all my toes. I've been sitting all day. If not for Fola who insisted that he drive me down here, I don't know how I'd have survived that Ikotun traffic, holding the wheel with all that exhaustion between my shoulders. The guy is so good to me," Jackson said, rolling his shoulders.

"Good man," Ian said. He had always been amused by how much significance Jackson placed on his workers merely doing their jobs. "I hope he left with the car; you're riding with me."

"Yes, it's the official car," Jackson said. "I'm thinking of giving him a raise. Remind me, Honey."

"That would be, er, nice. Not necessary, though."

"Come on. He deserves it. Do you know I fired my PA today?"

Ian's eyes widened. "Celestine is gone?"

Jackson nodded, hands on hips, rolling his pelvis. "I overheard him today in the toilet saying to someone on phone that he still found you bringing me lunch and flowers at work really, really funny. That maybe the man-to-man madness had stopped, since you didn't come today. And that we were both sick in the head."

"Gosh."

"I'd been tolerating his rudeness and ineptitude for so long." Jackson sighed. "I didn't realize he was daft, too. No, not near me. He should go somewhere else they are not sick. I was still dealing with that. Then these Asian—"

"Sit, Babe, come, sit. Your Chinese dare not miss giving you the contract. You've won it already. Forget Celestine, too. You're here. I can now breathe." It was silly, but it was close to the truth. Had he felt this way in their courting years?

"I look like hell, right?"

"Work stress has got nothing on your beauty in my eyes, Jackson. Sit."

Jackson sat, the pins in the lapels of his suit flashing. "You look so handsome," he said, and Ian blushed. Jackson leaned over and pressed the roses to his nose. "Mmm, they smell sweet. And these candles! You hopeless romantic." He jabbed playfully at Ian's tight arm. "Happy anniversary to us, Ian."

"Happy anniversary to us, Babe." Ian poured the drinks and, as they toasted, said, "To a never-ending journey of life", which Jackson echoed, smiling tacitly, because life was love, too. To love was to live. They sipped.

"Tomorrow is Valentine's," Jackson said. "I won't go to work. You have me to yourself."

Ian made a mock-cynical face. "Oh, if I have to tie you down."

Jackson laughed, and Ian felt like recording it. It was a laugh that was as piquant as it was unfettered, like a celebration song. He had laughed that way after the birth of their fourth child, Okenwa. On Okenwa, they had agreed to end all surrogacy deals. The carrier had snatched her final check from Ian's hand, breathing a sigh and literally running out the door. Her excuse? She had other clients, and Ian and Jackson in particular had had enough of her services. Ian and Jackson smiled. The only reason they had kept her that long was because she had beautiful features and an intelligent head. Nice genes there. Their hold on her also came from the insecurity of not having had much hope beforehand. How many men like them could afford surrogacy? How many men lived in dark, patchy parts of Nigeria? How many men even went to school, even had the chance, let alone the choice, to create their own lives as they wanted it? Ian and Jackson knew this. This was the reality of their privilege, the terrible life they had narrowly missed.

Ian signaled to the waiter walking towards them that they needed some time alone yet. They were eager now, as though they were long-lost friends who just bumped into each other after many decades. They started, naturally, talking about the memories that stood out for them so far, memories hitherto too stark for them to air.

"This has never happened before. This is our first anniversary in Nigeria, without our friends crowding around us and interrupting our moments," Jackson said. He sipped from Ian's cup.

"Yes, babe. I think it's scintillating."

"What kind of a man are you anyway, always remembering to mark our anniversaries? Real men shouldn't have time for all this." Jackson's tone was luminously acerbic.

"I have told you before: you emasculated me," Ian said. "Besides, I knew the drama that would follow if I forgot." He drank from his cup. "Do you remember that hot day on our way to an event at Ajah and a vulcanizer shouted, 'You

165

are following *onye ocha*. Is it because he has a Rolls Royce?'
?''

Jackson laughed again, even more loudly. "Yes!"

"You never told me what 'onye ocha' meant."

"You want me to put Nigeria on 'see finish' for you? Don't worry o; you don't *have* to know. And it was not an abuse. Aunty Oby calls you that, so it can't be an insult."

"Oh." Ian made a mock pout. "Now, I'm hungry. Let's eat."

"You remember our first penetrative sex, when I painted you a muddy brown?"

Ian flinched. "Gracious Lord! Yes. I remember. Golly, Babe. I will never forget how you stared right back at me, unblinking as I cleaned myself up. It was so uncharacteristic, such bold staring, in all my years of sleeping with people, that I got stuck."

"Oh, well, I was actually getting myself ready to educate you in case you were not already educated, Mr Mississippi." Jackson was laughing.

"I know! Did I react to the situation like an educated person then?"

Jackson let many silent seconds tick past before saying, "Yes. Yes, you did. You leaned over and kissed me and said to me, 'Babe, let's go to the bathroom but don't let that stop this moment. Stay with me.' " Jackson paused and traced the edge of his cup with a well-manicured finger. "I will never forget those words. 'Stay with me.' "

Ian clutched his hand, briefly. "Just as I won't, either."

"Let's cut the histrionics," Jackson said. "I didn't miss your first reaction, though." He crossed his eyes. "You *were* disgusted."

"I have a highly expressive face," Ian said, feeling a twinge of helplessness.

"It's natural to feel that way. Do you remember when you wanted to propose, that same momentous February at that resort in Bournemouth? You knelt and your hand was shaking and the ring fell and rolled down the patio into the hibiscus and we had to crouch in the dirt to find it." Jackson was held in-between paroxysms of laughter.

Ian's hands shielded his face. "Oh, ho! I remember! God, I was embarrassed."

"My most vivid memory of you ever." The nostalgic gleam in Jackson's eyes was almost fluorescent. "You looked so helplessly cute. Another that comes close is that summer we spent in Newcastle, when you climbed one of those godawful trees to taunt me and started pulling me up to you and my hyctophobia made me want to cry and you said 'Hey, I'm stronger than a tree' and you asked me to lean against the bole and hold up my face to you and I did and you leaned over me and kissed me on the brow."

"I had to. It calmed you." Ian rubbed his eyelids.

"It calmed me. And I suddenly imagined that I was up there with you. Inside the tree branches."

Ian reached across and tucked his fingers into Jackson's. He swirled his Senõr with the other hand. "My clearest memory is us darting lawn-sprinklers at each other at the home in Westminster. You were screaming like a girl and I said it. Remember?"

"Ah, I did. And that was the last day you used that toxic-masculinity line on me."

"Oh God! I realized how much of a jerk you had said 'Yes' to!" Ian was jerking with laughter.

"Really? Then the one who married that jerk got lucky." They stared at each other over the candles. "I wouldn't say it was all luck, though," Jackson added, narrowing his eyes in the candlelight. "The years have been turbulent, really turbulent." He paused. "I just believe, no matter how many or few the chances or privileges there are, people who want to marry will marry."

"Hmmm. Yeah." Ian rubbed his jaw. "And people who want to stay married will stay married. It depends on *what* we call 'marriage', anyway."

"You are damn right, my Knight."

Ian's bashful eyes swept towards the doors. "You are a gift."

"Do you remember how your Aunt Maggie used to scowl at us from the balcony?"

"Jesus, I do!"

"And then she said, 'You will soon stop this passing-phase thing, you hellbound assholes.' "Jackson sipped from his glass and stared into one of the lit candles. "So American a word to use. She had her mouth like she swallowed something rotten in there. I felt so sorry for her."

"I, too. She lived quite an unhappy life."

They burst into laughter.

"Jesus! Babe, do you remember your birthday in Birmingham, that small whirlwind that happened in the lawn tennis court? We were playing and I was beating you."

Jackson clutched his throat in relived horror. "That devil! It snatched my racket from me and spun me around."

Ian collapsed on his seat, drawing stares. But Jackson didn't stop talking. "You kept telling me to calm down, that it would soon blow over. And I kept on shrieking."

"Jesus of stormy winds!"

"Swears, Honey, I still insist it was your Auntie Maggie who sent that monster to us."

"Her possibilities were limitless anyway," Ian said, wheezing from mirth. "My mom used to refer to her as 'your father's fatal sorceress'. So there!"

"I would agree that witchcraft does exist in *obodo oyibo*." Jackson dipped his head. "I'll never forget the night we forgot to keep the children's room locked and went out to sit on the swings under the stars and Dera crawled out of his cot and we didn't know until we heard his cry in your study."

"Damn. We rushed in and he was sitting at the foot of my desk, my laptop on his leg, his foot trapped, his nose and eyes running. He kept bawling. I was so mad."

"Yes. We found out he had ripped up all your research papers. Your laptop was heavy and still connected to its socket. Anything could have gone wrong. I leaned against the door jamb. I wondered if I was about to lose my boy. He held out his small arms towards you, still hollering. I knew you were pissed already when I heard you use the F-word. You almost never used that word. I was frozen where

I was. I was expecting you to do something uncharacteristic, like yank him up and smack him, and I was hoping you would not. But you kicked your laptop off his leg. And you did not do it."

"I was too enraged," Ian said, "not even about the papers he ripped up. But smack him? There was no way I would have corrected him with that kind of language. He was already hurt, anyway; what would more pain achieve? He would never do it again, knowing firsthand how much it hurt."

"True," Jackson said.

Ian pushed aside his glass. "Babe, what if that laptop had crushed his bone? We would have lost our baby, our sunshine, just like that? What if he had got electrocuted? What would we have done? What would have become of us?" He shuddered.

"Parenthood is a marathon," Jackson said.

Ian sighed. "I swear."

There was silence around the candles, around the flowers. Then Ian said, "Hey, do you recall the morning we were changing their diapers and this same Dera said "Dadas" and sprayed urine all over our faces?"

"Jesus! No, I don't want to!" Jackson bent over and then rocked backward on his chair, waving his hands. "I thought I reeked of ammonia for weeks! Babies can't be homophobic, we know, but that Dera boy was a very homophobic child."

Ian's shoulders bobbed up and down. He thought of recording this, this moment with Jackson at their thirty-second, so he could play and play and play it anytime

Jackson was busy at work. He could even send a copy to their children. Ian had insisted on their Igbo names, which Aunty Oby had sent at each of their births, in carefully sealed envelopes. But for that, Jackson had seemed determined that nothing of his culture would be exhibited in their home.

"Wasn't it Dera again who took my money to take a girl out in school and buy her a dress for his prom night?" Jackson said with a small chuckle. "I had to speak some responsibility into him. If you want to take a girl out, then you make your own money, rather than stealing people's. That's honor."

Ian rubbed his face with both hands. "Oh boy. That boy's teenage rebellion was insufferable."

"I think the problem was that we pampered him too much," Jackson said.

"You mean *you* did."

Jackson shrugged. "Hello, don't point fingers. You know what we went through to have him. And I thought we were stopping at two. Tochi was the mature big sister; she at least rejected all the fawning."

"Ha-ha-ha-ha," Ian sang-song, waving a finger. "Not so resistant if you ask me. She had issues with me bringing you breakfast in bed. She would stand at the door, arms folded, nose turned up, and say, 'If Daddy can have meals taken to him in bed, why can't *I* have meals taken to me in bed, too?' and stomp away before any of us could reply. Do you recall how she kept my credit card and used it six times when she was in college? 'Girls' Trip' or some other monstrous thing."

"It was for their summer camp stint. You didn't spank her the way you spanked teenage Dera, though." Jackson crossed his eyes and stuck out his tongue.

Ian laughed. "I was already becoming a Nigerian. Okay, let me avoid that hard fact." He hid behind his glass.

Jackson tittered. "Tochi had always had her own troubles, too, anyway. You remember when she was in high school and had to go to detention for pulling out a classmate's hair in class?"

Ian mused. "Was it the Frisbee accident she had with that blond boy?"

"No. It was the day after their open day, after we visited, and this particular classmate was laughing with his group at the back of the class and telling them how he had been confused seeing us walk down the corridor with the principal, because he didn't know which one of us was the 'Mummy' and which was the 'Daddy' and could Tochi please enlighten 'the rest of the sane world' on the conundrum. She replied and the boy hit her and she hit him back."

"I remember." Ian chuckled. "I also remember what our daughter said in response. Her class teacher—may he rest in peace—wouldn't stop reciting it."

"Who could forget such an epic reply? You also aped her a lot." Jackson said, a shimmer in his eyes.

Ian raised a hand. "Wait, let me see if I can still mimic her." He cleared his throat and pursed his fingertips. " 'Okay now, I didn't know being a woman automatically means you *are* a mother, or that producing a child as a woman makes you a 'mother'. But today is the day you begin to live, boy. Take this wisdom. Motherhood is a *role*.

Motherhood is like fatherhood. A responsibility for your child's welfare. A friendship with your child. Being there for your child's emotional, psychological, intellectual, biological and social developments. I do not lack these. Now if *your* own mother had done a wonderful job raising *you*, we wouldn't even be having this conversation. She couldn't do to you in years what my parents have done to me and my siblings in months. *Education.* So shut up and learn that there can never be a vacuum in a universal happy family. Oh, save your thanks. And take that lesson home to heal.' "

Jackson was hyperventilating. "The way that girl speaks!"

"She took that from me, I guess."

"Is this a joke? She took that from *me.*"

Ian raised his palms. "I surrender. I surrender."

"Speaking of the girls, you must recall that summer we flew to Atlanta to see Mmesoma in law school and we found her crumpled on her kitchen floor, crying, hugging that fluffy pink teddy bear of hers, and her ex rode by just then on his power-bike, and leered at the glass door. Just before that red-Mohawked punk could flee, you strode right out to the back and grabbed him and punched his mouth for breaking our little girl's heart." Jackson's eyes glowed. "Did you know his teeth flew out?"

Ian's cackle was high-pitched. "I was younger and thrumming with the energy of being in a foreign place. Plus nobody messes with my baby girl and just scoots off like that. Nope. You know I'd always held a grudge against Americans anyway, even if I envy them and speak like them sometimes, so yeah, I packed some that night."

"You were such a lion."

"For what that's worth, I gotta look out for my pride." He mimicked a roar and said, "Simba!"

" 'Mufasa' was more no-nonsense, methinks." Jackson rolled his eyes.

"'Mufasa' it is then," Ian said. He beckoned to a waiter. "Excuse me, do you have *oha* and *akpu*? Jeez, I hope I pronounced those correctly." The waiter looked horrified, but not as horrified as Jackson looked.

"Wait, Honey, what the actual fuck!"

Ian's face settled into a stage-cast solemnity. "I hath already made thee the promise to stand by thee for always and make thy dreams come true." He laid his hands across his chest, fist-clenched and wrist-lapping. "I crosseth my heart and hopeth to die."

Jackson shrieked with laughter. "Jesus Christ! How are oha and akpu my dream that must come true?"

Ian cocked his head to one side, locked eyes with the boy behind Jackson, winked and said, "I just know."

"You goofy old ass! Wait, what the fuck are you looking at?" Jackson turned around. "You and that boy have conspired against me, right?"

"Well, yeah. He was right here with me while you stood me up. He saw the anxieties you put me through, waiting for you, even after all these years together. His parents did roughly the same thing to him. They left him there and did other things. It's only natural that I formed a bond with him, and now you gotta mind your language before him."

"Come on, stop the emotional blackmail. I raised four healthy, successful, respectful kids already. And it was because *you* raised my legs first. Don't tell me about minding language!"

"Oh, you mean, 'we *razed*'—"

They cackled into each other's face, like hormonal teenagers on their first date. The boy guffawed, too, while his parents gawked uncomprehendingly. It was exciting, how the intimate knowledge of words easily brought about the malapropisms of words.

"But, really, let's face it," Ian said. "They may have come from both of us, but Babe, they took all your Nigerian fighting genes! Have you seen how stubborn each of them is? And remember, around last month, Tochi did exactly what you did. She fired her receptionist for saying 'fags' when CNN was running on the lobby TV and they were talking about queer rights in Liberia. She wrote 'for gross incompetence and insolence towards customers, and for discriminatory acts on the job' in the dismissal letter."

"What are you talking about? Almost all of them did what *you* did. Okay, we don't know what Okenwa will do yet; he's still obsessed with his photography career in Paris, but at least we know about the rest. Only Tochi married another Igbo. Mmesoma did what you did: she went and said yes to a Hausa gold merchant in Kano. And Dera's tenacity is from you. Did you see the way he chased his wife before she finally said 'Yes ooo, yes, I will!'? Poor Yoruba woman."

Ian threw up his arms. "Okay then, I give up." He looked around at the tables. "There is no winning with this guy!"

The diners gave them benevolent, perseverant glances. The boy laughed. Ian winked at him again. It was curious, wasn't it, how children participated in things with a rapt zest as if they understood them, things that they actually do not fully understand yet, tender tendrils of knowledge that would sprout into deja vu in their future. He turned to the utterly entertained waiter, who was still standing and watching, and made fresh menu orders for two. It was a familiar, easy exercise; he knew what his husband ate.

"Now," he turned back to Jackson, taking his hand again, coyly, cajolingly, "Babe, are we still going to see Aunty?"

Jackson held out a pair of lapis lazuli cufflinks. They glinted in the restaurant's dipped light. "Yes, we are. But first, happy anniversary to you, my darling. I love you."

Ian took the cufflinks and enclosed them in his palm. He peered at his husband, the words gripping the base of his throat. "I love you."

•••

Akin Adesola Road in Victoria Island glittered as Ian drove into its interiors, bobbing his head along to the Dennis Osadebe song streaming out from the stereo, the only song apart from Fela's run-run Afro rhythms that Jackson allowed from Nigeria's music industry to get within an inch around him. He was ridiculously excited. They were driving to Jackson's aunt's home, a cream bungalow seated behind violet-colored gates, buffeted by allamandas with which the kids had loved gloving their fingers during summer holidays. Anytime they were in the country, they drove there for lunch, for dinner, for family time. "Rerooting ourselves in Nigeria," as Jackson wryly called it. This was their first visit without their children. Even though this left a gap in his spirit, Ian couldn't wait to see the woman again. The last time they visited was four years ago; it was for

Dera's wedding, which had claimed Lagos Island's biggest event hall.

As soon as they turned into Mogaji Drive, Ian pressured the accelerator. The ATM booths by the roadside became a dizzying blur and Ian could no longer feel the under of his thighs. The golden street light flowed like water on their bodies. The speed dial pin swung up alarmingly.

Jackson gasped. "You'll get us killed!"

Ian guffawed and twisted the wheel just in time to miss a stray cat. There was a screech. The black City swerved drunkenly. Jackson started laughing, too. He shrieked while Ian yodeled to Dennis, the safest he could come without mangling the lyrics. Jackson slapped the back of his head, still caterwauling. They whipped past the Ugonna Shawarma Spot and the dubiously named Free Citizen Security Company. Ian rounded the bend into Aunty Oby's street too sharply, without looking or switching on the signal. A block-industry truck lunged at them at full speed. It was too late to veer the black City off the warpath. The truck slid off the lane. Jackson screamed. The truck driver rained expletives on them in loud Yoruba, looking back from his high window as the truck vroomed off in plumes of exhaust smoke.

They arrived at Jackson's aunt's house in one piece.

"Honey, what in the name of Paul Walker's 'Fast and Furious' did you pull that stunt for? You could have rammed us into a tree!" His excitement was obviously still humming all over his joints.

Ian chuckled, unhooked his belt and landed a kiss on his nose. "What a way to die. On the night of our wedding anniversary."

177

"You're a foolish man!" Jackson was throwing his head against the headrest, his shoulders vibrating. "Why am I *not* furious at you? I should be pounding your chest right now! You know if I had my car here, it would be your ass losing this insane race, right?"

Ian cocked his head sideways. "Ha, I wouldn't bet on that."

"Good! Try not to get us killed next time. You are not the only one eager to see my aunt, you know?"

Ian tapped his fingers on the sleek wheel, the skin of his arms covered in early age dots, a feature that left him rather sour at Jackson's still-seamless, barely wrinkled skin. " 'Where we love is home, home so that our feet may leave, but not our hearts.' "

"Aw. That's Wordsworth, isn't it?"

"No, Holmes. Oliver Holmes."

"I don't know who the fuck he is." Jackson giggled. He freed his torso from the seat belt and made to climb out, but Ian gestured to him to stop. He jumped down from the car and went round to open the side door.

"Seriously? You won't stop doing this?" Jackson covered his face and eased out of the car. "Thank goodness the children aren't here yet. I'd have choked from embarrassment."

"And who says they are not already here?" Ian pushed the door closed. He was only pulling Jackson's legs. It was a commercial season. Their children would be too busy with Valentine's Day staff package deliveries and enclosures to bother about them. Yes, they had called that day, in scattered successions, to wish them a happy anniversary.

178

But Ian knew better than to expect a family gathering. The older the children grew, the looser the family's physicality became. Even though the phone calls and Skyping never ceased, Ian wanted their children to remain children: clingy, needy, dependent, *present*. And he knew Jackson wanted the same.

Before Jackson opened the porch door, Ian felt a prescient thrill run through him. He lingered. He was not as surprised as he would have loved to be when Jackson walked in ahead of him and gasped, "They are here, Honey! My kids are here."

"What?" he managed to say.

"Happy anniversary, Popman and Daddy!"

Ian felt like he had felt at the quiet church in Blackpool, while he stood before the minister, waiting for Jackson to walk up in his white lace jumpsuit, a fleecy cloud of utopia and friends surrounding him, the halo of a dream brightening true. It was like waking up from a beautiful reverie to live it. His children were standing in the living room, the biggest cake Ian had ever seen placed on the table in their middle, bottles of wine around it, the chandeliers above gilding every surface. Multicolored balloons bobbed downward from the ceiling. Jackson hugged everyone, crying and commenting on their "foolishness". Ian couldn't move at first.

"Popman," Mmesoma said, walking up in her flared Ankara knee gown. "Are you going to stand there and not say 'thank you'?" She hugged him, closely, burying her forehead in his shoulder like she used to do as a girl, and Ian felt heat behind his eyes. When he watched her court session clips on CNN, imperious and severe in her pencil skirt suits and erudite oratory, even as his chest swelled with pride, he often failed to remember that she was still his soft, small girl. He wrapped his arms around her. The rest came up to greet him. Tochi clung to him. He laughed, pleased that they could still be like this. It did not happen like that in novels, in the fiction he himself wrote. Ian shook hands with Mmesoma's and Tochi's husbands—they pushed anniversary-present envelopes into his hand, bowing and grinning. Already smiling, he hugged Dera's wife, Ikeola, his secret favorite of his children's spouses, who held onto his neck and quipped, as she normally did, "See how you're glowing like a *soji* boy! If not for how far *ni*, Pop-in-law, I would have snatched you from Jay and taken care of you the matchless Yoruba way!"

"I love you bitch, but a thousand of you can't take my husband from me." Jackson folded his arms and turned up his nose. "Proved and foolproof."

Ikeola gasped, unclasping her hands from Ian's neck. "You challenge me! Look at your son's cheeks! Wonderful, because I used the Oduduwa method for him. Calm down and let us take care of your husband. We Lagos babes no dey waste time o. We are general caretakers. I don't even know the charm Dera used to key me down!"

"You wish," Dera said to general laughter. His light handsome features made him a smaller version of Jackson. He was a US-trained nurse on a government-sponsored child mortality rate alleviation programme in Nigeria. He left what he was doing in the kitchen and, napkin in hand, walked up to enfold his Popman in his arms.

Jackson rolled his eyes. "*Wahala* for whom was not embraced o, or how do you youngsters say it again?"

"Your colloquialism was too English, Daddy, but I will embrace you again, to make up for Chidera's slackness," Tochi said, walking over to him.

"Oh, pardon me, is someone jealous?" Dera said, still locked in Ian's embrace.

Tochi laughed. "Come off it, D., you're such a fish." She clasped her palms around Jackson's shoulder.

"I know I'm a fish, Ms Harvard engineer. That's why only I make the best salmon dishes in this family. Not even any of you girls can stand against me in a kitchen contest. It's not by constructing bridges and highways," he turned to Mmesoma, "or speaking *supri-supri* Latin in a courtroom."

Tochi gasped, her lips rounded in a mock-stung surprise.

"My son takes after me," Ian said.

Mmesoma giggled. "Who's deceiving this one? Because you can boil water and drop Maggi in it, we won't hear word again."

"Ha, my children have totally become Nigerians," Jackson said with great cultural sorrow.

"Don't mind him, Daddy," Mmesoma said, claiming Jackson's other shoulder. "He's just a braggart. What can he cook?"

"Women!" Dera wept. "Everywhere you turn, they call you names. Their loyalty *nko*? A mirage is more reassuring. You're just lucky, Popman. I can't begin to report Ike to you. She doesn't only call me Big Head, she also calls me Small Yansh."

"Don't spoil me in front of my crush, young man!" Ikeola protested from where she sat straightening the greetings cards mounted around the cake. She turned to her sisters-in-law's husbands. "Have you people seen this man? I cannot call my husband 'Small Yansh' again. Is he not my husband, eh? Is he not my husband?"

The men obliged her, "He is your husband."

Ian laughed and shook his head. "Son, if I tell you the names your Daddy calls me these days, you won't call me lucky. His tongue is more ruthless than that of a woman."

"Like we don't know anyway," Dera said slyly, glancing at Jackson.

"Just stay put there with your Popman, or else," Jackson threatened. "Goodness, I miss my darling son. Okey would never forsake me like this." His face crumpled in mock tears.

"Please don't mention that silly boy," Mmesoma said. "When was the last time you held him? He didn't come for my wedding. Didn't show up for Tochi's. Same for Dera's. He doesn't know my children at all. He wouldn't even come down to Nigeria for this. All he knows how to do is TikTok apologies that have absolutely nothing to do with me. 'Mmeh-Mmeh, sorry, won't you pardon your darling kid brother?' *Aarghhh*. If I slap him."

"Whose side are you even on, babe?" Ikeola said, rising and walking towards Mmesoma.

Mmesoma paused and chewed her lower lip. "I don't know," she confessed and everyone laughed again.

Ian said, "Let my daughter be." Ikeola said nobody was holding his daughter. She said her brother-in-law would come home, and that he would make it a surprise visit; they chatted daily on Instagram.

Jackson tried to hide his eagerness. Mmesoma rolled her eyes. Ikeola laughed.

"Speaking of surprise," Ian said. He waved his hands around the cake and cards and wine and balloons. "How did you guys manage to do all this? We told nobody we were around."

"But you told Auntie," Tochi said.

"And Auntie told Dera," Mmesoma added. "You know she couldn't keep a word from Dera. If she were still able to menstruate, I'm certain Dera would be the first human being to hear all about her cramps."

"*Aargh*, that old witch," Jackson said.

"Easy now," Ian said. "You guys are not going to turn your spears on my in-law, are you?"

"The jealousy in this family is as thick as winter snow, Popman," Dera said. "It's not anybody's fault that Auntie Oby loves me. That *everybody* loves me. The spoiled brat gallivanting around the globe wouldn't even come close."

"Hold your husband, *bae*," Tochi said to Ikeola, "before my sister and I pounce on him. He should watch what he says about Okenwa. Is this playing?"

"I release him unto you, Great Coven. That's how he turned my son's back on me. That one does not even want me sleeping alone in the same bed with my husband; he must come and wriggle in-between us. And it is always 'I want to play ball with daddy', 'I want to wear wristwatch like daddy'. I had never seen anything like that. I have gone and dumped him in my mother's house. More undisturbed time for me to draw up my lesson plans at home. And do other things. Thank God I've weaned him. *Hei!* No child born of me or not will disrupt my love life and work o. I leave the father to you, though. Do with him as you please, O Witches."

"You went and dumped my baby pumpkin in your mother's house?" Mmesoma said. "Babe, you are The Witch."

"Lady Morgana," Tochi offered. Ikeola rolled her eyes. "Don't demote me. I was thinking I was Dahlia."

Jackson turned to his daughters, his eyes widening in horror. "I hope none of you have done that nonsense to the rest of my babies. Where are my grandchildren?"

"Daddy, the triplets are away in their boarding school," Tochi said, amusement stretching her lips. "When it's holiday time, you will see them, either here or in London."

"Haba, Daddy, Ify is too old to wriggle in-between Bala and me on the bed." Mmesoma laughed. "Relax. She just sat her pre-high exams. She and her brother will be home when their current school term is over. They ask after you and Popman every day, and I think we should all Skype sometime."

"Their boarding school has such provisions?" Ian asked.

"Popman, you should visit Nigeria more often," Tochi said.

Ian smashed a hand on his forehead. "What kind of a granddad am I? I should have known about that, instead of just longing to hear their voices all the time I'm away."

"With all your mouth," Jackson fired at his son, "you went and put a witch in your house and in your bed."

"Love is a crazy thing, Daddy," Dera fired back. "Popman married *you*."

"Babe, the shade," Ikeola said, then went and stood protectively next to Jackson. "You will eat your words, we promise you."

Ian coaxed Dera out of his arm and nudged him towards Jackson. "Go on. The pretense is over. Just go and hug him and tell him how much you missed him. You know he loves hearing it."

Dera mimed a mock reluctance and shuffled towards Jackson, who turned his nose away dramatically. "What is it?" Dera sneered. He turned to his sisters and wife. "Excuse me, please." The women shifted. Dera placed his arm around Jackson and drew him close. His youthful tallness made Jackson a head shorter than him, so that Dera's beards grazed Jackson's head. "Don't be jealous. I grew up practically clinging to you. We went everywhere, played squash together, did everything together, two of us inseparable. Now that it's my Popman's turn, don't be jealous. Okenwa that is now clinging to you used to be glued to Popman. Children change."

His brothers-in-law hummed their support from their seats. They gave anecdotes from their own lives, fathers they used to be distant from, towards whom they now drifted often. Mmesoma sat next to her husband and shut him up with a kiss. Tochi covered her husband's eyes from behind with her hands and said she wouldn't remove them until he supported her Daddy.

Jackson finally turned to his son, stared into his eyes and hugged him. Ian grabbed a bottle and said they all needed to "pop to the truce". They laughed. They joked, as always, about the self-indulgent bump of his belly and asked

Jackson not to be stingy with the details of his own firm-tummy routine. Jackson said their Popman would never be caught *not* eating. They laughed again and again.

"You're looking dashing, Jay, how come? I almost didn't recognize you when you walked in. My crush is really a sweetheart, isn't he, taking care of you like this," Ikeola said.

"Don't start, bitch. And get my grandson for me before I leave Nigeria, or I'm clawing those pawpaws down," Jackson said, swatting at Ikeola's breasts. Ikeola shrieked.

Dera excused himself to the kitchen. Mmesoma went in with him. Ian ambled over to Jackson and slipped his arms around him, whispering sweet nothings in his ear.

"All this talk of food is making me hungry o," Ikeola said, rubbing her belly.

"Wait," Ian said. "Where on earth is my in-law? Where is Aunty Oby?"

•••

Aunty Oby came out of her room in the back wing and stood at the entrance of the swinging-curtain living room door, beaming. The bead curtains clacked. Jackson walked over and embraced her. She rocked him from side to side as though he were still a twentysomething-year-old, and said stuff in Igbo. Ian watched them, feeling his heart expand, the way it had expanded all those years ago after Uncle Nwabunike had rejected Jackson's visa offer, saying firmly that he did not need a passport, did not need a visa, because he was not going to attend the wedding, and Jackson had turned to Aunty Oby and said, "If anybody thinks I will bend over before they can accord my life its due respect, then I cannot help it. I will get wed to Ian whether you are there or not." And Aunty Oby had surprised them—surprised Ian more, really—by procuring her visa and flying to be at the wedding.

"Onye ocha! *Oyibo!*" Aunty Oby called when she saw him now. Her hair was turbaned, but she could see the specks of gray in its edges even from where he stood. He walked forward and enclosed her in his arms. She was shorter than he remembered, and even though her fairness had dimmed only a tone darker, her face was now a wrinkly mass, with dark patches around her eyes. She had on mascara, and Ian suspected that to be Ikeola's handiwork. He held her delicately. She felt brittle, not the sturdy, fleshy weight he had hugged at the wedding reception in Glasgow. Ian's throat clogged at the ineluctability of the human withering, at the fact that people will die.

"I've missed you," he said into her neck.

"I've missed you, too, my nephew's star." She tightened her arms around his body.

Ian could tell that this, this homecoming, was the most final, the most significant, and the most memorable for them, for him in particular. At Uncle Nwabunike's funeral three years ago, he and Jackson flying into the country several days ahead, Aunty Oby had welcomed Ian's condolences with a curt, shaded nod. She had also merely shrugged, morosely, giving no exact guidance, when Jackson asked her how much Uncle Nwabunike's age group demanded for the funeral rites. She dispensed remnants of that aloofness towards him on all those visits he and Jackson made in the past for "family time". Her brother had died without forgiving Jackson for what he did to the name of the family, which they had been carrying like a precious, fragile clay pot. Her brother had died with sorrow in his heart and bones. And Ian had felt like a heartless marauder. But now, with her arms so tight around him, things *were* different. She had come to remember—and even expect—his smell, his essence, his inability to break under any pressure. She had come to see him as not only sexual, but as more than sexual, emotionally present, just the right complement for her nephew, who was as intransigent as a rock.

Jackson handed the Cadbury love bars and Bacchus wine hamper they had brought with them over to her. She collected the basket and said, "*Eziowku?* My child, you know I can no longer eat these sugary things. I will take only the wine, for my heart."

"You don't eat it at all then. When your great-grandchildren are on holiday and come visiting you, you can give it to them," Jackson said, patting her on the shoulder gently. "We brought other things for you; they are in the boot. We'll send the children to get them later. But first, let's eat. I learnt Dera has been reigning in your kitchen all day."

Aunty Oby laughed. Ian could see her youth in her open-jawed, open-toothed laugh. "I heard all the things you said to my boy. *Hapu ya aka biko.* My first husband has *kuku* forsaken me and is now running after French girls."

Ian and Jackson laughed.

Aunty Oby raised her nose. "Ah, that aroma."

"Dinner is ready!" Tochi called, clapping as Dera started bringing out casseroles and covered trays, his brothers-in-law going over to help him while the girls moved to the vast dining section and seated themselves at the table, Aunty Oby sitting at the head, flanked immediately by Ian and Jackson.

"Popman, I hope you can now eat pepper," Mmesoma leaned over and whispered to Ian. "Dera's wife has taught him the most potent culinary Yoruba evil. I tasted that *ofe nsala* in that kitchen and water came out of my eyes. No kidding. Today is the day we fully understand that expression: 'you are in hot soup'."

Ian's mouth went slack.

•••

The lunch went well. The garri was finely made; it didn't scratch the throat. Only the nsala soup made Ian suck too much air into his mouth while his eyes watered. They all clapped him when he chewed the last of his chicken and ground the bones with his teeth.

"Eaten like a real *agu*, my son," Aunty Oby said, to everyone's laughter.

"Yoruba people and people who marry them will not kill my husband for me," Jackson said, reaching across the table to rub Ian's chest.

Dera said, "Popman is getting used to it. My in-laws have a Yoruba saying that translates to, 'When a mouth does not eat pepper, the soul that carries it will be small.' I don't know why you people are not grateful to me o."

"Don't mind them, baby," Ikeola said. "There is no pepper at all in this thing! I was about asking you that why did you not put pepper!"

"Why don't you and your husband kuku set our tongues on fire so that we can have peace in this place?" Jackson said.

189

"Your English is becoming so Nigerian so fast, Daddy," Tochi's husband, Somto, said.

"This infectious city, my dear, this infectious city," Jackson said. "You can't come to Lagos and leave without it staining you."

"I agree with you." Somto laughed. "The other Monday morning on my way to work, I spent close to an hour arguing with a *danfo* driver over who was to blame for breaking my trafficator. I couldn't believe myself when I finally reached my office. Back in Onitsha, I would have quietly driven away."

They laughed. Ikeola and Tochi rose to cut the cake. They left it in large pieces, which Aunty Oby avoided because of the icing. Ikeola nudged away the sugary edge with the knife and gave her the plain cake on a plate. Mmesoma ate hers directly from the cake tray. The men stuffed their chunks in their mouths. It tasted like sweetened strawberries, they said.

•••

Aunty Oby sat where she was at the dining table, her turban removed, her head now leaning back, while the girl who lived with her and ran errands for her stood behind her chair and parted her hair into sections that she was now oiling and getting ready for tiny but not-so-tight cornrows. Aunty Oby's eyes were closed in a tranquil half-sleep. "I would have asked you to do it instead," she had said to Mmesoma and Tochi, "but even you people go to Ikeola's hairdresser to make simple braids and throw away outrageous money." Bala, Dera and Somto sat around the center table, on the purple Persian rug, playing whot. Ian had joined earlier, but they had booted him out. Too many "Checkup!"'s against him. He retorted that he would rather go and play his dear old golf at Ikoyi Club and that none of the boys should follow him. He found his way to where his husband and Ikeola were, by the pillar in the alcove next to the hallway leading into the rooms. They were playing Ludo. Ikeola was beating Jackson silly; Ian could see most of the reds and blues from Ikeola's corners piled outside the board, while Jackson's greens and yellows were still roaming the squares frustratedly.

"You cheat," Jackson fumed. "You brought all the goddesses of your land to tackle me."

"Ahn, ahn, Jay." Ikeola laughed, clearing yet another counter. "Small Ludo game and I will be disturbing Osun, Oya and Moremi? It's too much *na*. It's not that deep."

"Whatever. I'm sure you're cheating in one way or the other. And I won't let you off that easily. You'll see."

"Don't beat my Babe too much," Ian pleaded.

Ikeola giggled.

Jackson jerked around. "She wouldn't dare!"

"Where are Mmeso and Tochukwu?" Ian asked.

"Right here, Popman!" Mmesoma clacked through the curtains, holding an iPadOS to her chest, Tochi right behind her with the speakers.

Dera looked up from the Queens card in his hand. "Time to call that brat?" he asked.

Mmesoma nodded. "Time to call that brat."

Aunty Oby opened her eyes.

"Get me my glasses, *nwa m*," she said to the girl behind her.

"Mr Bala, I don't even want to hear anything from you. When I arrive in Nigeria, that caftan is the first thing I'll be collecting from you. *Mon Dieu, it's magnifique.*"

Bala laughed. They were all crowded around the dining table, the iPadOS switched to Skype and propped directly in front of Aunty Oby, who was now wearing her glasses. Ian and Jackson sat on her either side as before. The rest clustered behind her. On the screen, Okenwa peered back at them, trussed up in a crew-neck sweater and a beanie, his expression a seemingly frozen sneer. He had Jackson's humor and full lips. The few traceable features he had to Ian were his nose and sharpline jaw. Occasionally, he sipped something from a paper cup. He blinked at Bala, expecting his answer. Bala laughed again. "*Ba wahala.* No problem," he said. "You're welcome to do that. But I will also collect something from you, as atonement for not coming to our wedding."

"*Je suis pret.*" Okenwa laughed. "We'll fix that."

"*Nwoke ruru unyi n'ala ga-echeriri idozi ya,*" Somto said, wagging a finger.

"Ah, Big Bros!" Okenwa was laughing. "You haven't forgotten that?"

Somto gave a belly chuckle. "*E ji m aka n'ichetara, oh?*"

"Of course, I've been mastering them by heart," Okenwa said. "I'll clean things up. Thank God I've been consulting my jotter o. Na so you go just catch me."

"*Kedu, nwanne?*"

"*A di m mma.*"

"*Pfft.*" Tochi rolled her eyes. "You only know the simple courtesies. Are you an Igbo man like this? You should be ashamed of yourself." "Leave me o, Aunty Mascara-Eyelash. I'm not the country that chased my parents out of it and made us lose touch o."

"Oh-hoo, *negodi*," Aunty Oby said, darting an accusatory glance at Jackson. "Your Daddy should have at least been speaking Igbo to you people while growing up. But he was just as disinterested and still is."

"Aunty!" Jackson protested. Ian squeezed his arm gently to tell him that Aunty was right. Jackson pouted. He poured himself some water.

"It's all well. *Sha* come home," Tochi said.

"Why?" Okenwa sipped from his cup. "Big Sis missing me already?" Tochi glared. "I most certainly do not! To think you did not even come for our first baby's dedication."

"Thou art funny, sister," Mmesoma said. "Is it someone that did not show up for weddings that will now show up for child dedication?"

"Ah, Mmeh-Mmeh, you're there? *Comment ca va?*" "Stop calling me Mmeh-Mmeh. I'm now in Nigeria and I go to all these public markets with people dragging billy goats up and down and the word has taken on a whole different meaning."

But Okenwa brushed all that aside. "See how *splendide* you look! Look at your hair!"

Mmesoma tried not to blush. "See, eh, Okey, I would have said something to you right now, but because our dads and Auntie are here, I'll restrain myself. I owe you one."

Okenwa laughed. "You owe me *two*, sis, remember? That summer holiday when I dropped something in your cup and you stood on the diving board and stretched out your arms and started singing Mariah Carey in a terrible off-key?"

"*Tufiakwa,*" Mmesoma said, laughing hard. "How are my nephews and nieces? I've missed them." "They are fine," Tochi said. "They also miss their Uncle Okey who only calls and never comes."

"Aw."

"IK threw her child away, though," Mmesoma reported. "She said he was disturbing her and her husband's romance."

"IK is a witch, what did you expect?" Okenwa said, gesticulating to shape a flying broom.

The girls laughed.

Okenwa said, "I miss you, sisters."

"Aw," Tochi and Mmesoma said.

"Not you slying me, ma niggur," Ikeola said. "You told me not to let them ever know you miss them."

"*Excusez-moi.*" Okenwa groaned. "I know I'm supposed to be a proper society man, not showing soppy emotions and catching feelings and all that. Your babes used African power on me. They cast a spell that made me say that. Drag them, not me."

"Which spell, fool?" Ikeola doubled over, laughing. Okenwa was also laughing on the screen. "Sha don't reveal the date you are coming. You said it is going to be a surprise."

"I won't, babe." Okenwa blew a kiss. "Where is that husband of yours? I hope he has not run off to be chasing stick-man drawings on the streets o. The times are desperate. Stay woke, please."

"*Uchu! Onye ara!*" Dera burst out. Everybody dissolved in laughter, even Ian who did not understand the cusswords.

When Okenwa found his breath, he said, "Calm down, bros. Your babe na better babe na. Have you seen how she slays on IG? Even Jay Z is following her! So you don't know that any other babe is a stick-man drawing?"

"Your mouth there! Spoilt brat! *O sighi gi n'aka.* Between you and me, whose eyes can't stay in one place? I'm sure every girl in that place knows the number of hairs under your boxers!"

"Uh-oh, *nna*, that hurt." Okenwa had his face zoomed across the screen, his lower lip pushed out to accentuate the intensity of his mock-hurt expression. "I don't even sleep with a babe twice."

The men broke into hollering, slapping each other's palm and back.

"See? See what I'm saying?" Dera said, turning to them. "He still thinks he's a teenager." He faced Somto. "*Nwanne*, when next you guys have your language lessons for him to have knowledge, can you please insert some deep proverbs so that he will reflect and have wisdom, too?"

Somto couldn't even reply. It was Bala who did. "Leave my in-law o. Let him marry at his own pace."

"You, you no marry? You no marry?" Dera asked.

"I'm older than he is."

"And obviously more family-oriented," Dera said.

"Nna, free me," Okenwa said. "We can't all be the same. At least, I speak with the family three times every week. By the way, go and open a WhatsApp account, *biko*. Your Facebook Lite messenger app na stress. I can't send you clips from my trips. Who uses Facebook Lite these days anyway? Do you know that I covered the foreign students visiting the Eiffel Tower from Africa last week? See? I can't even send a VN."

"I won't. I don't have time to be chatting. You can send them to my mail; I'll definitely see them there."

Okenwa passed his hands down his face. "IK, how do you cope? This man is the most stubborn I have ever met."

Dera shook the flat of his hand. "Just disrespect me one more time and see if I won't slap you through the screen."

Ian caught Jackson's eye. "When will they stop bickering over things like this?" he asked.

Jackson smiled reminiscently into his glass. "When we stop," he muttered.

"Chill, bro!" Okenwa said, reeling away from the screen, his body jerking. "Just don't come home. I will first punch all that nonsense attitude out of you before I beat you mercilessly at football."

"Ha, bro, don't think it's like before o," Okenwa said. "I've been practicing with some boys from the PSG FC here o. These *hommes* are the real deal. I'll just be dribbling you all over the place."

"*Nekene*. What's all this mouth? Bayern Munich nearly tripped you guys at Champions League. It's not by dribbling o. Can you give a killer shot?"

"Why not."

"We shall see."

"I miss you, too, bro." Okenwa drew from his cup again, smirking.

"Don't make me curse you, this child."

"I love you, too, bro."

Everybody screamed, and despite himself, Dera chuckled. "*Mumu*-boy," he said. "*Abeg, comot.*"

"Okey," Ian said.

Okenwa leaned forward, his eyes darting from one parent to another. "Hey, guys, why are you both looking so *peng*? Is Nigeria actually still the hellhouse you ran away from to get married?"

"That's right, son," Jackson said, a wry grin cracking up his face.

"*Epouvantable*. You are brave, dads, going back there."

"Okey, we are fine," Jackson said. "Really, Daddy? I'm worried, honestly. I'm really worried about you. If they touch you—"

"*Detends-toi, mon fils,*" Ian said, raising a thumb. "Nobody will see us and behave like an animal."

"Okay, Popman." Okenwa smiled. "Did you like the cake?"

Jackson gasped and held a hand to his chest. Ian said, "I should have known. Who has 'A Very, Very Gay

Anniversary to the Straightest Couple on Earth' written on their parents' anniversary cake?"

"The silly bum had the package couriered here this morning," Mmesoma said. "And had the nerve to be telling me that I should make sure it got to you in one piece. Like I'm a glutton or something."

"Oh, my childhood rankles," Okenwa said, playfully crossing his eyes. "You didn't let any of my lunch-pack sweets live. Your sweet tooth is a none-sparing terrorist."

"That's true, Soma," Tochi said. "Don't argue."

Okenwa laughed.

"Do you now have a stable relationship?" Ian said. "*Non*. I wish I could choose a different sexual orientation, honestly. Boys shouldn't have this much stress. Look at you and Daddy. You guys are the real troupers. You stick together like glue."

"You can find your own glue and stick to it," Dera snapped. "You're probably just too distracted."

"That's not it, big bro." Okenwa dipped his eyes, fidgeted with his head warmer. "Daddy, how did you guys do it? I can't keep a girl for two months."

Jackson glanced at Ian; Ian smiled. It was still evident in Jackson's eyes, even after all these years, the secret prayer that Okenwa was at least bisexual. Ian shared this prayer. It was the reason they kept on trying even after three kids; they had hoped to have at least one non-hetero child.

"You youths of today are something else," Jackson said. "A relationship is not something that just happens, readymade. It takes mutuality, efforts, changes, growth, evolution. No relationship that stands today is perfect, or

198

was ever perfect. But it takes two to tango, and it takes two knowledgeable people to tango *well*. It is never smooth. It takes forgiveness, and more. And you don't just *own* people. Or dictate to them *how* to love you. Do you love them because of what they do or don't do? Love seeks no permission and no explanation for itself." Jackson paused. "Your Popman did his homework. He knew what he wanted and it helped him to know just how to get it. I did my homework, too. I knew what I needed and what I wanted and how to tell them apart. Do your homework before you enter that class, boy."

Okenwa sighed. "Now you sound like my postgrad teacher."

"Listen to your Daddy, Okey," Ian said. "You and I will have a heart to heart soon." "Okay, Popman."

"I might even come up there. I have some research to do."

Okenwa's eyes lit up. "Seriously, Pop? *Tres bien!* I can show you to Jacqueline then; she's my current. She is one of your biggest fans. She can't stop talking about 'Miles to a Cathedral'."

"Aw," Ian said.

"Yes, Pop. She'd be over the moon to finally get an autograph. What are you working on this time?"

"A Roman archaeology story told through the eyes of a Caribbean. No, the protagonist is not straight this time." Ian felt a stretch within him, watching his son's excitement. In their middle childhood, at bedtime, when he sat between their beds to read them Enid Blyton and Charles Dickens, Okenwa had always been the last to drop off, his eyes glittering and mirroring every emotion shared from the

199

stories, sitting upright while his siblings yawned and said "Good night, Popman" and pulled the duvets over their heads.

Okenwa laughed. "Better. Make them pansexual and non-binary, please. I love it when people open a book and are shocked."

Ian and Jackson laughed.

"When fathers and son finish laughing, maybe my husband can finally locate me," Aunty Oby said to general chortling.

Okenwa licked his lips and drew closer to the screen, inching his mouth forward and forward as though he meant to kiss Aunty Oby through the flat screen. "Baby *m. Asa m pete. Ola m. Ugo m. Omalicha.*"

Aunty Oby glanced at Somto. "You've really been working!" she said. Somto laughed and ducked behind Bala. "*Kedu, obi m?* How are you faring? How are strangers treating my husband? How is work?"

"I'm okay, Gran. Everything *o mma.* But why are you fine like this? You alone fine like ten people."

"*Hapu m o,*" Aunty Oby said, a tired look in her eyes. "Don't sweeten my mind. All your siblings are here with me. When are you coming home to see me?"

"Granny, it will surprise you. *E kwere m gi nkwa.*"

"Come back soon, Okey, my son. Your grand auntie needs to see you before she joins her ancestors."

Okenwa pulled a brow, and Ian saw a flash in that expression of Jackson when Jackson's manager gave an unpalatable report. "Stop saying that, please, Gran"

Okenwa said. "Mon Dieu! You're meeting my wife and kids before you do anything awful."

"Then come home and let me see them. Your brother and sisters have given me great-grandchildren to look after. Look at me. Look at my hair. I am old. I am too old."

Okenwa's eyes misted over. "I have said I will come home. You dare not go anywhere before and even after I do that."

Ian bristled; he found blackmail in Aunty Oby's words. Her well-being was poised in a way that would inspire guilt rather than care. But he forgave her; after all, there were such cultures all over the world: children forever serving parents' wishes from a place of contrition instead of a genuine care. "*Ngwanu,*" Aunty Oby said. "My *chi* is wide awake. She has heard you. Besides, I need to teach you your grandfather's poetry. Sopuruchukwu never wanted to learn it from him."

"*He* wanted me to learn statistics and business management so I could oversee his firms," Jackson murmured. Ian nudged him again to ask him not to argue with Aunty Oby.

On the iPadOS screen, Okenwa's eyes brightened again. "Poetry! I'm definitely coming home soon then." He peered closer. "Granny, did you fix lashes?"

Aunty Oby looked away bashfully.

"Which one of you is responsible for this sacrilege?" Okenwa glanced around, hiding his laughter. His eyes settled on Ikeola, who was guiltily arranging her blouse straps. "I know it is you, of course. Ms IK the fashion fad!"

"Please, shut up there," Ikeola fired back. "I simply blushed up her cheeks and combed out her—"

"It's your iniquitous chutzpah for me," Okenwa said. "You want to send my Grannie to hell fire."

Aunty Oby held her temples, rocking back and forth. "You children won't kill me. It's nothing, *di m*, it's just mascara. It's not eyelash. I feel younger with it. I feel—what's that expression again?—'takeaway'."

"You are supposed to be a Christian, Gran. Your body is the temple of God. I even learnt that you inked your husband's date of passing across your upper arm. That's tattoo! Don't let those Godless people derail you in that house. Send them packing. Only my dads should remain."

"Jacqueline no dey wear eyelash?" Ikeola asked.

"Jacqueline is young," Okenwa retorted.

"Not you unrepentant fornicator preaching against sin. It's your hypocrisy for me. Go and marry."

"Oh shut up." He glanced downward at something and gasped. "It's almost 2pm here! Guys, I gotta rush. I have a tour capture at the Seine River by half past two. Some students from Tanzania want to see Notre-Dame. They have been booked since Christmas, December last year. Catch you guys, later. Grannie, I won't forget my promise. Daddy, take care of yourself for me. Popman, I'll be expecting your call. Dudes, you dey all right. Babes, bye-bye. *Je vous verrai bientot.* See y'all soon. I love you!"

They waved goodbye. The screen went blue and blank. Jackson patted Aunty Oby's shoulder and murmured, "*O ga dimma*", which made Aunty Oby smile. Mmesoma gathered up her iPadOS and went to keep it. Tochi sat next to Ian.

The men drew away. Bala picked the family photo album and leafed through it quietly. Soon, Somto and Ikeola went to join him. The girl behind Aunty Oby waited patiently for Aunty Oby's signal to resume her work. Ian and Jackson locked eyes, communicating words no other human could hear.

Soon, the atmosphere charged up again when Dera said he felt like treating Ian to another "real Nigerian dish", since all Jackson ever gave the man were chicken and chips taken from inside a fridge and defrosted in a fancy microwave.

"Come, Som-Sugar," Bala said, drawing Mmesoma away. He passed the album to Somto. "Let's go out to the backyard and finalize our Valentine's Day's plans. If our parents start now with Dera, we won't leave here."

"You have my blessing, son, but don't plan too much and tear my daughter's dress o," Jackson called after them.

"*Chineke*, Daddy, I'm actually happy the kids are not here to listen to that!" Mmesoma said.

"*Kai.*" Bala hurried out with an abashed face, Mmesoma in his wake.

Somto glanced at Tochi and got up slowly, a predatory glint in his eyes.

"*O gini?*" Tochi said. "Don't even start." "Too late, omalicha. I have started." He chased her outside.

"Small Yansh, won't we go and do our own, *bayi*?" Ikeola held up her wrist imperiously.

"Stop calling me that!" Dera swung his hands to his derriere and made a mock-hurt face.

Ikeola dragged him out, laughing. Aunty Oby chuckled. Ian watched her closely. This was her dream, exactly, only unfolding in the dimension she once never allowed herself to think of. She couldn't be happier, surrounded by love, by warmth, rather than by flimsy unbendable things. The girl stretched her hair, glistening strands of gray, and twisted it deftly into fronds. Ian watched them climb up her occiput, to rest as a tapering bunch atop it, its tails flaring.

"What do you call those?" he asked the girl, pointing at the cornrows.

The girl tilted sideways slightly, her ear turned as if to catch his words carefully and correctly. "It's called *Shuku*, sah."

Shuku. *Gray Shuku.* That was when the title came to him, the Nigerian story about Nigerian people he had always wanted to write—if it *was* his story to write. He would start it after this one. He would have to pay more attention to how Nigerians talked, their colloquialisms, their brand of pidgin, *their* English.

He straightened up on his seat and faced the window opening out into the backyard, the cool night air fanning his face. "Hey, guys, one more thing: what in God's name is 'yansh'?"

FATE

IN THE BEGINNING

Aliu and Shehu grew up in the same compound in Lagos; children laughing and running into each other; face-me-I-face-you rooms mixing songs from door to door, a clash of Di'ja and Tope Alabi and Ice Prince on Sundays, and a more strained clash on Saturdays—between who bunched up the half-dry clothes hung out on the single line (because they needed to spread theirs) and whose clothes had been bunched up. Anyone living in such a compound became quickly familiar with the clanging of a pot's lid in one room, heard in another; the smells of different soups mingling; rosters drawn up for sweeping the yard and cleaning the bathroom and the toilet, often sparking arguments and sometimes scuffles; people lining up in a shambling queue in front of the borehole tap; too many I-better-pass-my-neighbor generators growling at night; mothers bathing their children in the open yard, especially if they were new tenants avoiding a bathroom that was thick with the smells of strangers. Aliu and Shehu were two of those children. As their mothers turned their reluctant bodies this way and that, dragging the rough-fibred *kain-kain* over their faces and other parts, Aliu and Shehu would gaze at each other's nakedness, for too long, until the soap lathered into their eyes. Usually, they still prised their eyes open and peeked through the burning foam. They watched Chinese films in each other's single apartment. They went to the same *ile keu*. Sometimes, they used the toilet together,

205

a makeshift zinc affair with a white ceramic pit in the middle. They would take old custard buckets next to the toilet, then sit and wince and eject. But they never said a word to each other; always watched each other with sealed lips, as if united by a common knowledge too grave for speech. Until a day in December, when they sauntered back home from a Jum'at service, side by side, and Shehu limply swung out his hand to touch Aliu's.

"How old are you?" he blurted.

"Nine," Aliu promptly answered as if he had been waiting for the question, for any question at all. He smiled. "You?"

Shehu told him he was seven years' old. His hand dangled too close to Aliu's palm. He kept it there, their little fingers interlocking. He wanted to say more, like pass a comment about Aliu's eyebrows, so full and so arched that they looked cosmetic, but he didn't know if Aliu would jerk his hand away. They walked the rest of their way home in that loud silence, both of them smiling, speaking with their minds, only disconnecting sharply when they walked through their compound gate and found Shehu's mother washing clothes under the *agbalumo* tree.

The following week, as they walked homeward in the same noisy silence of their minds, Shehu made the first move again.

"I don't know the name of your school," he said. "They did not write it on your bus. I always look when it comes to carry you."

"It faded." Aliu gnawed at his nails. "Providence Kiddies Nursery and Primary School."

"Okay," Shehu said. The silence roiled in their ears. "I attend Regal Lives."

Aliu had walked past him and was already walking ahead. Shehu watched his small derriere wig-wagging. Desire swelled inside his underpants. Panic gripped his ribs. They had neared the compound gates when he lunged forward, jammed a kiss on Aliu's cheek as he had seen the woman do to the man on "Sound of Music", and dashed towards his mother's room, his heart thumping. They didn't speak again after that day. They never spoke again.

Because that same December, Aliu traveled from Abuja with his family, and they never 'came back'.

•••

YEARS HAVING GONE BY (1)

Aliu waited impatiently for Saida to come out of the mosque. It was too sunny for September. The wristwatch seemed to cling to his skin, and he wanted to yank his embroidered cap off. He longed for a cold bath.

"Saida!" he shrieked just as she stepped out of the mosque's walls—with all his dreaded foes trailing behind her. He hated it when she let those guys follow her, because it meant he wouldn't be able to walk alone with her. He wouldn't be able to escape their taunts, which were like knife incisions driven on his heart.

"*Naaam!*" Saida replied. "Hey, why were you shouting my name like that?"

"He has missed his wife *ni*, what else!" one of the guys replied.

"Which wife?" the others asked. "Does Aliu look like a man? Do two women marry?"

They laughed and laughed and laughed.

"Whatever," Aliu said. He wished he had not flicked his wrist so smoothly and rolled his eyes so silkily. He sucked his teeth and looked away. This had them in even wider stitches.

"But *yan dauda*," one of them said, an irreverent boy from upper Gwagwalada who had the disconcerting habit of popping bubble gum while the frustrated alfa enunciated Allah's expectations and the *jaanama* that awaited the *kafieris*, "why do you like behaving like a girl, *ko*?"

Aliu stared back at him, wondering what would happen if he slapped that stupid smug face already. He hated this guy. He didn't know his name and he didn't care to. Why did people assume that you "liked" something because you did it often?

"You people should leave my Aliu alone," Saida said, adjusting her hijab, raising her thick, perfectly shaped eyebrows but smiling.

"Are we holding him?" Bubblegum Boy giggled like an idiot. "*Zo*, Boy-Girl, are we holding you? Can we hold *haram* like you?"

They slapped each other on the arm and howled.

"Don't call him Boy-Girl."

Saida's voice came a little too limp, a little too late. Their laughter climbed decibels. Aliu watched them, then turned and started walking away. This was why he stayed close to Saida. Perhaps if he stayed close to Saida, he would finally transcend himself. He would finally acknowledge her crush on him. He would finally become a *man*. And no longer a *haram*, an abomination. But he detested the way she was sounding now. It was goadingly deceptive of her. It was as if she was the starter of the joke on him, rather than an accidental participant.

That night, when he went to her flat because her roommate was away in Kaduna and she said she hated sleeping alone, she placed her hands on his chest and asked, as if she had only just noticed the stiff furrows on his forehead, "Aliu, what's wrong?"

"Nothing."

"Are you staying the night?"

"Yes." Why was she asking obvious questions?

They ate bread and boiled eggs, and drank tea, which Saida had quickly boiled earlier when there was light. It was the season of their final exams. After studying their lecture notes for a while, they lay on the mattress on the floor, Saida in loose bed pants and a camisole, Aliu in his Boxers shorts and singlet because of the heat. Silence pushed its way into their middle on the mattress. After a while, Saida spoke again.

"What is it?"

"What is what?"

"*Haba mana.* Seriously? You're sulking."

"I thought I said 'nothing'."

Usually, they rehashed the day, went over something silly somebody had said in class, which student had devised new ways to dupe his group members of the group project money, which new lecturer was said to be sleeping with the cleaners. Or they could just be playing hip-hop, their secret sin, on Saida's Bluetooth speaker, the volume turned down so low they could hear only the muffled beats, until they drifted into a tired, bored sleep.

"Is it because of what Ibrahim said?"

"Ibrahim is a fool." Aliu shook his head and turned his back to her as he usually did when he was in her bed. He felt like farting. Although they were buddies and sometimes undressed in each other's presence, he didn't know how she would react to such flagrant intimacy. A sudden memory flashed across his mind, too brisk to be clear. He waited to see if it would come back. If it would loom into déjà vu. It didn't. Only his fart made a growling, disappointed sound as it crawled back into his stomach.

•••

YEARS HAVING GONE BY (2)

The rain might have stopped, but its consequences had just begun. The woman walking confusedly from teller to teller stepped her mud-caked soles on that same spot again. That was the fourth time. Shehu was tired of living like this. Lagos was full of *poto-poto*. Why hadn't she wiped her soles clean outside? He grew up here, yes, but Lagos was mad, he agreed. Lagos was hectic, furious with commerce. The people there would never be caught strolling through their activities. It was almost as if they woke up in the morning every day, pressed a "don't-stop" button on their bodies, and charged through the day like unassailable robots. It must be the reason his friends who lived in more insular suburbs outside the state called Lagos "the city that never sleeps". And nobody ever said a genuine thank you. Why should they? Everybody saw it as his duty to clean the bank's floors. People should not be thanked for doing their duties, especially for which they were paid, yes, but was it a new attitude birthed by staff imperialism, or had it always been like this but he just hadn't noticed it when he was growing up—this thankless, songless attitude towards low-level staff in office?

"Excuse me?" a familiar voice called behind him and, for a moment as he turned, he expected to find full, curvy eyebrows and a clean-shaven head. But he saw a wig, large eyes, and a small pretty face; the eyebrows were sickeningly near-invisible. He gripped the mopping stick, fighting the sensation to reel to the floor.

"Yes, ma'am. How may I help you?"

The woman's eyebrow shot up, a rapid tic that said she was startled and impressed. He had watched enough eyebrows flick up like that when he spoke English to know by now that people didn't expect him to speak English at all. It was simply preposterous. He peered into her face, giving in to an aching interest. It was his tenth month in the bank and he knew almost every customer by face by now. The old man who tottered delicately towards the counter, looking around helplessly for the right teller to attend to him, his wizened hand quiveringly clutching his withdrawal slip, and stopping at the end of the queue at the deposit desk, until Shehu walked over and, taking him by his shriveled shoulders, guided him to the withdrawal queue, every time. The petite, severe woman who must be a teacher and who always complained, pushing and pushing at her thick-lens spectacles, that the teller was delaying her. And then that couple who ambled in on Fridays, just an hour before closing time, wearing sneakers and hoodies, holding hands and giggling loudly and stroking each other's beards and staring into each other's eyes so obviously that Shehu wondered if they realized they were still in the confines of Nigeria. But he had never seen this woman before. He

211

peered harder. Perhaps he would remember her in that tight hallway of his face-me-I-face-you childhood home. A memory that must have magic in it, because it had refused the erasure of years. Perhaps she would know somebody he once knew there. Perhaps she was even that person's sister! Not that he had known any sister back then. Forget the nonexistent brows. From that sharp timbre of her voice that pierced the years into his mind, to those large, large eyes, there *had* to be a link.

She was speaking. "Hello. Hello."

Shehu snapped out of it. "I apologize, ma'am. You were saying?"

"Could you show me to the toilet? I'm pressed." Shehu was nonplussed for a moment, because a nebulous glimpse from the past had seared its way into his mind at those words, "I'm pressed". He led her towards the steel-walled toilets and stopped at the main doorway. She mumbled her thanks and disappeared. Shehu retreated to a corner, next to a water dispenser, his mopping stick forgotten in his hand, his mind racing through the thicket of his memories. He wanted to catch that watery image that often overwhelmed him, especially at night, an image that never quite solidified into a whole sense.

She came out so soon that Shehu imagined that she had peed through her skirt without lifting it. She walked past him, nodding gratefully at him. He acknowledged it with a shrug.

"Sorry to disturb you, ma'am."

"Okay?"

"Did you by any chance live in Oshodi?"

"Oshodi? No."

"Or around it?"

"No."

"You sure?"

A sigh escaped her curvy lips. She glanced at her wristwatch. "I said no. Actually, I've come from Sagamu. I came to see my uncle. He was the one who sent me here. I'm going back to Sagamu today."

"I'm so sorry." What was he thinking? That magic was real? What had he expected from meeting her? A sort of time travel? Reincarnation? He must have read too many indigenous novels. "I was really hoping you'd somehow know someone I used to know."

"Oh?" Her eyes lit up, a voracious luminosity that instantly filled Shehu with foreboding. "Who would that be?"

"Nobody you think." Shehu supported his words with a guffaw that stopped short of a jeer. He watched her eyes dim slightly. She reminded him of his friends and neighbors, people who often looked at him and exclaimed, "Ahn Ahn! But you are too fine not to have a girlfriend *na*! People wey get face and body like yours, na girls dey rush them!" They spoke expectantly, as if giving him the chance to recant, to say he had been joking about his celibacy and that he sneaked girls into his room when his mother was either out or dead asleep. But he always received their insinuation with a serene, amused smile, doing nothing to goad it, doing nothing to dispel it either. Which left them frustrated.

"Oops! Sorry!" The lady glanced at her watch again. "But I have to move. The traffic in this your Lagos *ehh*, na die!" She looked at her wristwatch again and fled.

He gazed after her with a faint sobriety spreading up his throat. He knew she would face worse when she stepped out. The whorl of traffic along Falomo would be snarled with the one coming straight from Obalende and the whole place would be a jumble of fenders and bumpers and broken side mirrors. Horns would blast from gasping cars and multi-dialectal curses would rise to stain the dusk. And passengers would be trapped in immobile buses for hours on the road. He felt an overpowering urge to have a car at that moment so he could drive her to Sagamu and spare her all the horror.

He got home that evening, drained of any will to even cook, hoping his mother would have made something. But he met her in front of their apartment, sitting next to her half-empty stall, eating soaked garri. He greeted her, and she greeted him with news that was both shocking and exciting.

"Your father's brothers have asked you to come over to Abuja. They called me just now. *Alhamdulillah*. They are finally hearing our situation. They want you to come and start university there. You will be living with them and leaving from there."

She said those words in a rush, as if she feared she might not get much out before the coughing seized her again, and all the years collapsed around his shoulders. Like deflated weights. He stared, in the undecided light of evening, at the empty bottles of kerosene on the kiosk, the bare basins of garri and beans, the dusty packets of cigarette, and recalled all the days he worked as a petrol-pump attendant to eke out a living and source for his JAMB registration fee, and how he had spent most of it on his mother's bronchitis, and on feeding them both. His throat burned when he recalled his sense of immaterialism before he found the bank cleaning job, how he would avert his eyes towards the petrol pump, ignoring the taunts of his old schoolmates who were living large on yahoo-yahoo money and who had driven in, in their Benzes, to get fuel. And now, without even needing to put forward his earnings at the bank, his dreams were taking shape, hardening into reality. And yet, as his mother hugged him and asked him to take a spoon and join her, because this was joyful news and the garri had sugar and groundnuts inside it this time around, he wondered why he couldn't share her triumph, why the eventual realization of his yearnings did not feel like a dream come true.

•••

MOVING AGAIN

It took several botched attempts to convince Aliu that his hopes would always be stillborns. His body would never cooperate with his mind. It chose his heart instead. He could never do what Saida wanted. And it hurt. It hurt more because Allah did not want what his body was doing, yet Allah had used this to torment him. Was it to test his *iman*? This Friday, he joined the throng of the faithful on the treeless field, in the sweltering heat, to spread a mat and touch his forehead to the grass-spangled soil and mumble prayers and adulations. His scalp burned underneath his cap; the dry stickiness left his back and arms itchy. Their imam had insisted that it was there, out there on the burning plain, that the Mecca sun had moved. Nobody complained. They simply filled their kettles and washed their orifices and limbs. Aliu lifted his head, blocked his ears with his thumbs,

215

shut his eyes and prayed. *If Mecca chooses to make me suffer, then I'll find my own Mecca and live.* The people knelt, leaning leftwards as their imam did, and counted their beads. Aliu's movement was slow. He remembered a boy. Perhaps the boy was him, perhaps the boy was not him, but he remembered a boy, and the boy did not even have a beard. He longed for the beardlessness of that time, of childhood, because the absence of beards and of tallness brought fewer expectations and, therefore, less responsibility. He would do anything, sit, kneel, bow under any sun, to go back to the setting of his dreams. But he knew it was a wild wish. He was stuck here with his father, the same one who had sent for him and his mother from Lagos. He didn't have the full details but that was what his mother told him: that they had once lived somewhere else and that Aliu's face had been brighter, his smile quicker and fuller, in that place.

The imam cried out, "*Atahiyatulillah wasolawatu watoyibat!*"

The faithful picked up the cry, the response, the *asalam alieka ayu Anabi ya warahmatullahi robarakatu, asalamu aliena waalahi badilahi solihina.* But Aliu was silent, tight-lipped. He clutched his *tasbir.*

"*Ya* Allah, I miss the boy I used to be. I miss the boy I used to be. Help me go back. I am a liar. I am an unfaithful slave. Please. Help me go back."

The tasbir blurred in his hands.

•••

Saida persisted. The night before, she had grabbed the bull and its horns. And this had repelled him greatly. He had woken up in the dead of night, Davido still singing "Nwa Baby" on repeat on the Bluetooth speaker, to feel spiders crawling up his thigh. It took the utmost faith in Allah's protection for him not to scream and leap out of bed. When he raised his wrapper and looked, the spiders had become Saida's fingers. She was between his legs. She was grabbing the bull and its horns. But the bull was already dead, dead as Sallah ram. Aliu waited. It was haram, for a girl to make the first move, but he waited. He needed this haram. He needed to break God's shadowed face. But when the spiders climbed to the head of the bull, it revolted and re-died at the same time.

"*Auzubillahi!*" he said, leaping out of bed, although he was not sure it was not "Auzubillahi" he would have said if it had been another hand. That hand in the blur of his memory.

He scrambled away from her, muttering Al-Fathia stringently. She gave him a silent look, a calm disgust in her eyes. It was the same mien on her face when she spoke of hip-hop: that the spirit of Shaytan was in hip-hop, and that it was why people manifested under its spirit. And yet she never said no when Aliu connected to her Bluetooth from his phone. Boys like Aliu featured in everybody's gossip. But Saida still intoned, always, "*Aozobillahi shaytani rajeemi.* A man that has what you have on your body? *Salaam* is far from these kafieris." She said it with an ostentatious tone, as though to announce her pretense about her knowledge of Aliu. It was the same quiet distaste that sullied her unpretty features even further each time they walked along Galadima Road and saw the male couples carelessly concealed behind barely tinted car windows, necking and caressing. Of course, it was a normal sight. This was Abuja, the land of too much space and too much unreality, unlike Lagos with its loud, gritty brashness. They were walking past one of those cars that afternoon, their last day of final exams, Aliu carried off again into his usual reverie, trying to piece together, yet again, the skeletal lines of his elusive dream, when Saida slapped him on the back. He jolted awake. Hating Saida. *Another stillborn.*

His phone started singing Rema's "Ironman", a jarring wail of studio din. It was his mother. She was crying. Alhaji, his father, had just married a new wife and because she dared to make a fuss about it, he had thrown her out of his house, and promised to make life hell for both her and her "useless one son". It sounded like a poorly written story. Aliu pressed the phone to his ear and watched two boys skitter away in the distance, nylon kites lolling in their hands, fluttering in the evening breeze. He would always remember them as unsuspecting witnesses to his farewell, to his last moments in a place that rubbed dreams from his mind and replaced them with illegible pencil sketches. He didn't need a soothsayer to tell him this was another beginning. They were moving again. Back to Lagos. Where his mother's relatives were.

Beside him, Saida wondered.

•••

SLEEPLESS

Shehu stuffed his clothes and novels and Series questions booklets in his small bag, sat on his squashed mattress on the floor, his back pressed against the wall, and watched his mother as she snored up on her narrow bed. He found it surreal, far-fetched, the ability to lie prone, close his eyes and drift into oblivion. His body hummed with a weightless desire, yet he didn't want to touch himself. It was as if touching himself would leak his excitement and leave him flaccid and he would not be able to convince himself again. He would wait.

How possible was it to remember someone you met briefly only in childhood? The words from his childhood still rang clearly: "Your friend and his mother are no longer here; stop going to knock on their door. She said something about Abuja. You see that new tenant there? He is a soldier on the run. He has a long gun that he wipes every morning. Don't let him fire you with it."

Abuja. That was the touchstone of reality. His friend must be there. He would wait. He would wait until they got there. And then he would find him. He wouldn't stop until he found him.

His mother's delicate bedframe rattled with her snoring.

•••

THE DREAM

That night, separated by miles, their flashes and shadows finally took shape. They dreamed like spirits, spirits containing souls. They dreamed in a world that was not sane. They dreamed in a world that had never been known before. They dreamed.

"Hi."

"Hi."

"Is this real?"

"It's not. What binds us defies sense."

"Your face has not changed."

"Really? Yours neither. Look; the hill behind you is higher than you. It's as if we are still kids."

"We *are* still kids. We are in our young forms."

"*Lahi'lla. Gaskiya.* See, my arms are short. My legs, too."

"Mine also. And our voices are not broken."

"Gaskiya. True."

"I missed you."

"I felt the same way. I wanted so badly to dream of you, but your dream tortured me so much. It teased me with mere glimpses of you. My days carried you in them, in tiny pieces."

"I, too. Those eyebrows were the most defined picture I could see."

"These eyebrows made me find and lose too many people in Abuja. Nobody got a full picture."

"Same here. I was scattered across too many people. They thought I loved them. All they had was just a piece of me: my body."

"*Wallahi*, I'm jealous."

"Don't be. None of them meant anything like you. Like us."

"I know."

"What kind of thing is this, following us through the years and separate spaces and happenings? Why hasn't it faded off like it happened with all normal children of our time?"

"I don't know. I think it's just bound to be. Nothing visible links us. Yet, here we are. Bound by air. Bound by earth itself. If it wasn't meant to be like that, the normal thing would have happened. We would not even remember this much, you know?"

"I know."

"Do you know my most enduring memory of you?"

"No. Perhaps it would be mine of you, too."

Silence.

"Do you remember how we used to shit together?"

"*Allahu.* Yes."

"Come on. What's with the shy look? Are you embarrassed?"

"Yes."

"You know the smell of my shit."

"What?"

"You know the smell of my shit. You know me. You are not a stranger to me, so don't feel embarrassed, that's what I mean."

"Gaskiya... Same here. It's only in your presence I have ever been able to find it easy to unwind, to unclasp and be myself, without doubting anything even for one second."

"Oh, Aliu. Don't worry. One day, we will be free. Free to be. A new wind will blow into the land. It will come from another land close to *al-janna*. They will open their doors for us to come in and be free from this jaanama."

"That is my *duah*. My prayer every day."

"Come close, real close... No. Closer. Yeah. Now place your forehead on mine. Yeah. How do you feel?"

"I feel...at home. I feel rooted."

"Yeah. I've always dreamed about this time, this place, this us."

"I, too."

[Love is a tagless coincidence.]

"Are we finally living our dream then?"

"I think."

[They giggle into each other's face, mixing their breaths, squashing their noses together.]

"Are you still two years' older than me?"

"Ah...yes!"

"Good. 'Cause I'm still two years' short."

[He places his nostrils on Aliu's parted lips and draws a deep, deep breath.]

"Do you mind?"

"Never, Shehu. Nothing shall come between us. Not age. Not a country. Not life. Not death. *Insha Allah*."

"Insha Allah,"

[Shehu echoes, just before he flicks out the tip of his tongue, and caresses Aliu's upper lip with it.]

Time and space swiftly parted from each other and, in a sharp inward breath, the dream was gone.

•••

FATE

On the day they would meet, the sun turned the earth off-white. Their mothers had given their word, differently, without knowing exactly why: one said, yes, she remembered the way to the house in Oshodi; the other held her son's head to her bosom and prayed that he find all his heart sought in Abuja. Each son couldn't wait to trace his steps back to his idea of home and see what had become of it. Their dream propelled them. That dream splintered on the road: two journeys taken on exactly the same day, on the same route and at the same time; two long-distance vehicles roaring past each other on an empty road, one headed for Lagos, the other for Abuja, each son buried in his thoughts, distracted from the window glass, anticipating, not knowing that the other was sitting and dreaming in the passing bus.

The two buses missed each other.

ACKNOWLEDGEMENTS

I find no words rapacious enough to slip my parents in, these angels who bought the early books I read, the books that shaped my flair to write. They did not stop there—they proofread bits of my childhood manuscripts. They have loved and protected me like an absolute miracle. In my next life, may you be my parents, still.

My brother, my beloved *àtèlé*, the one I cannot replace, Oluwasegun, 'Atom Boy', who shares my working and winning days with me—'*Hanzo Hasashi*', guy, you rock!

I thank Oluwajuwon Adenuga, my beta reader, baby brother, friend all rolled into one. He was there to read the earliest, roughest draft, and to laugh and shake his head and say in his faux white American accent, "*Naw*, this doesn't werk."

All my Facebook friends who followed the Unfamiliar Love series in February 2018, the first public audience to some of the stories in this collection. You guys are priceless. I cannot trade you for anything. I cannot mention you, for an omission of one is an omission of all. Thank you for playing my keys.

My ablest draft readers, Ishola Abdulwasiu Ayodele, Ugochukwutubelum Nnamdi and Ola Halim—great men, thank you for being brutal and yet so excited in your responses. *Una be pesin true-true.* I am fortunate to have had you.

Booky Glover, who actually said, "I will talk to you only when you publish a book, you this stubborn child!"—thank you for twisting my ear.

Deji Adeyemi—I appreciate you for the early feeding of my soul, for your tender kernels of wisdom. They flowered.

Oluwafemi Bah—what would I have done without you? You wouldn't stop being a guardian angel for my muses. Willy nilly, I have written that book. Words fail me.

Manasseh Thomas, thank you, darling, for adding inches to how tall I am.

Jude Anuoluwa, you edited with so much wisdom, so much warmth, that I almost thought of you as my Earth Jesus. Your visit through those weeks scooped out the jewels in me. I keep saying it: you are too important; yes, *are*. I am still furious and confused and agonizing, and my tenses for you will always be in the present.

My students at D-Way Schools, who saw few of my tears when my manuscript file crashed and I had to start from the scratch; whose delight in my work is an inspiration on its own; who insisted that I let them help me edit while typing, and that I include their names among the characters. (Hey, Tolani, I put your name!) You guys were the reason I smiled to work every day. I will always love you.

To my Oga, the proprietor of D-Way Schools, Engineer Olagbaju, thank you sir, for providing an office filled with electricity, for letting me sit in your bouncy executive chair.

Mayflower School students (2005-2011), The Golden Set, thank you for calling me "Formable" in class and in the hostel. Thank you for reading my poems and stories and making them bigger than they were. I believed more stubbornly in me only because you believed in me first.

Obafemi Awolowo University English and Education class, the two departments and faculties that shaped my teenage journey right into adulthood, where the scales fell off my eyes (Great Ife!), friends and people from other departments and faculties, thank you all for saying, "One day, we will read you."

The Akinsanyas, the Jimilehins, the Adenugas (Tomiwa mi! Adunlolamiwa! Bless you, my beautiful sisters), the Sokoyas, my siblings, cousins, uncles and aunts who read some of my horrible childhood drafts and rubbed my head as if I had written the best thing ever, thank you. I was able to do this much because I was a child whose writing was blessed with your enthusiasm. May the families that have mixed beautifully into one another and become one never be scattered.

Thank you from my heart, Lorde Raphael. You are my *malaika*, an angel that shocks me.

Tigerwest Al Khalifa, the One who doesn't want to be named, but whom I shall name, because he is too good to me to escape this little recognition. I don't have the exact words to thank you for showing up for this project. For answering my sudden questions. *Dalu, nna.*

Adeyemi Dairo. I don't know why you are so good to me. Thank you for that text that had me yelling my bestie awake. Thank you for being shockingly awesome to me. *Mo dúpé gan-an ni.*

Busola Boyejo—you are a godsend. There are no words enough. Keep flourishing.

Tolu Lope, my beautiful Big Sis. May your joy never finish. Thank you for helping me carry my load to my head.

My own Squad! Ayofe the beautiful, my "ChummyChoCho", friend like brother; the elegant poet-albatross, Taiwo Hassan (TSoul!); my ever-sweet Grace; Emi mi; Pamilerin; Ola (Bobby); Christiana; Eniola mi—you guys are jewels. Thank you for pushing me when all I wanted to do was just lounge all day.

Thank you, IfeÁdigo Publishing Company, all the agents, all the team members, for bringing out my dream even better than I envisaged it. Your passion, patience and professionalism are top-notch. I am forever grateful.

Thank you, everyone who said, sent, and acted prayers and goodwill towards this book.

You guys are gods. Thanking you is thanking God, who has made me.

May your heartfelt prayers leave you happy and fulfilled. Amen.

ABOUT THE AUTHOR

Enit'ayanfe Ayosojumi Akinsanya is a young Nigerian writer. Born in 1994, in Ijebu-Ife, his mother's hometown, and raised in Sagamu, Ogun State, Nigeria, he is a graduate of Obafemi Awolowo University and a 2016 House of Levites "The Ready Writers" Campus Fellow. He was the first-place joint winner of the 2022 intercontinental "The Green We Left Behind" French Embassy Climate Change Project Prize for Creative Nonfiction, and signed a publishing deal through Africa's Arts Lounge Literary Magazine. His novel manuscript, "In the Half-Dark" (tentatively titled), was a major finalist for the 2018 National GTB Dusty Manuscript Prize for Full-length Fiction. He repeatedly made his mark known overtime as a recognized feature contributor in the 2017 Facebook-organized Microflash Fiction Contests, where he was named An Important Writer to Watch. An alumnus of Farafina and OkadaBooks 2018 GTB Writers' Bootcamp, his short fictions and essays have been published (as at the time of this book's release) in *Brittle Paper*, *The Kalahari Review*, *The Shallow Tales Review*, *African Writer*, *Livina Press*, *Eunoia Review*, *Fiery Scribe Review*, *Afrocritik*, *One Black Boy Like That Review*, *Nollyrated*, *Aayo Literary Magazine*, *The Yellow House Library*, *Arts Lounge Magazine*, and several more. His interviews have appeared in various top blogs and newsrooms within Africa. When he's not listening to music and reading poetry and human stories, he is arguing for repressed human rights, staring at nature or hanging out with his small circle of friends. He is always writing, but selects what to publish. This is his first grand publication. You can link up with him @Osumare_Ayomi on Twitter.

Printed in Great Britain
by Amazon